Love Letters from Dresden

A remarkable love story with a touch of magic

I0592756

Mark A. Biggs

Other books by Mark A. Biggs

Above and Beyond: 2nd edition (2014)

Operation Underpants: Book #1 Max and Olivia Series (2016)

Claudia: Book #2 Max and Olivia Series (2017)

Operation OBE (Over Bloody Eighty): Book #3 Max and Olivia Series (2018)

Love Letters From Dresden - A Remarkable Love Story With A Touch Of Magic: (2019)

St Mary's Dating Agency: Book #4 Max and Olivia Series (2020)

Operation Origami – The Ire of Claudia: Book #5 Max and Olivia Series (2021)

Operation Snowflake: Book #6 Max and Olivia Series (2021)

The Silent Trail (2024)

Love Letters from Dresden

Mark A. Biggs

Copyright

A CIP catalogue record for this book is available from the National Library of Australia.

First published in Australia 2020.

mbkbooks

62 Sunnybrook Ave

Warragul Victoria 3820

Australia

www.markabiggs.com

Dedication

Friends Craig and Jim

Disclaimer: This story is a work of fiction.

Book Cover

Cover design by Craig Braithwaite, aussiepics.

Love Letters from Dresden

Prologue

I was forged in another time, a symbol of love and fidelity, when myth and magic still roamed the world. As legend has it, I was formed from the same stones as the swords Caledfwich and Clarent on the isle of Avalon, one-part Caledfwich and the other Clarent, and when given in love, become one.

For the hundreds of years since my creation, I've travelled the length and breadth of the world and can tell countless stories of kings, queens, peasants and paupers – for I have accompanied many. But in this story, I start at the end, with a person of no particular importance who has worn me since she was a little girl of four. I was a gift from her father, a rough, dull, worthless-looking ring he found abandoned on the ground. However, because I was given in love, the present was priceless, and bore with it a touch of magic.

This beautiful girl grew to become a mother, and now in her twilight years, an elegant senior. Many would say hers was an uninteresting existence, but that's because they don't know the promise she keeps. As our time draws to its end, the hidden love letters will drift from memory, taking their secrets with them.

The wonderful tale I share is a tragedy, yet a story of fortitude and love, the chronicle of two exceptional women, their journey through war and a promise made and honoured.

My lady is sleeping, something she does more as age eats away at her energy, and in these winter years, the dreams take her back to darker times and places when unbeknown to my lady; I was walking beside her.

Come with me as we share the enthralling story of - Love Letters from Dresden.

CHAPTER 1

Amelia

Darkness envelops Amelia, lying unconscious in the bombed-out ruins of a building. The intense pain of a cramp that spasms in her leg jars her awake, forcing her clamped eyes open. It's difficult to concentrate and at first her vision is unstable. As Amelia awakens, her hazy mind cannot absorb what's happened. She blinks and the surroundings harden. She tries to lift her head, it moves, but unable to find the strength, she gives up. Closing her eyes, Amelia drifts back into unconsciousness. The next time she comes to, Amelia is aware of her dire predicament, sending fear rippling through her entire body. Panicking, she struggles to be free. Disorientated and unable to move, she screams out for help, but her efforts are in vain because words cannot escape her closed lips. Once more, the surroundings fade and Amelia drifts away.

Despite the bitter cold, fleeting rays of sunlight, peeking from behind grey clouds, penetrate the rubble to warm her numb face. This time, when Amelia opens her eyes, the panic and disorientation that overwhelmed her before dissipates, replaced by a dull acceptance. She is trapped under the debris of a bombed-out building. From her tomb she scans the surroundings; everything within sight is ruined. In the distance, a red glow is accompanied by the sound of a roaring fire. Lowering her eyes, moving them left to right, Amelia explores her prison, and to her horror, she is sharing it with human remains. Revulsion morphs into panic as Amelia wiggles frantically, trying to escape, but it's all to no avail. 'Help me! Help me!' she cries out, but nobody comes. *I'm going to die*, she whispers quietly to herself as tears swell in her eyes and dribble down her cheek. Amelia's eyes become heavy and, with no fight left, they close to await the embrace of angels.

The freezing chill from the coldest winter in recent decades deadens the unconscious body of young Amelia Huber. Slowly she awakens and, for the first time in many months, she feels warm and at peace. In the distance, the bright light of a lighthouse signals its invitation. Subconsciously, Amelia knows that if she gives in to the contentment enveloping her body, her life will be forfeited. Resigned to her fate, she embraced death as an old friend, offering an escape from the evil, suffering, and profound losses wrought by a seemingly endless war. A cosy light beckons and Amelia gently walks towards paradise, following an endless narrow path, lined on either side with beautiful flowers in radiant bloom and displaying all the colours of the rainbow.

In the distance and through her dreamlike trance, Amelia hears a man speaking; it is earnest, comforting, somehow familiar. Continuing to walk towards the light, Amelia sees that it's her father. Feeling safe at last and curious about what he's saying, she hurries to him. A devout Catholic, as a child, before she went to sleep each night, her father would read a passage from the Bible to her. He is reading from that book now and pauses, smiling at her approach, then continues.

'The people walking in darkness have seen a great light; on those living in the land of deep darkness a light has dawned.'

Amelia loved her father. "A daddy's girl," her mother would mutter to Hans Huber, as he soothed her despair at their defiant daughter, then sneaked a piece of buttered bread to her room when she had been sent to bed without dinner.

'Where are you going?' she would hear her mother ask crossly.

'I'm just going to read Amelia her Bible passages, my love. God knows she needs it.'

'Hans Huber, don't you go using God's name in vain with me! And I know what you're up to. You're spoiling her.'

'My princess, how could that be?'

'I'm no princess. Look at me, old and haggard. Too many years of hard work, and for what?'

'You'll always be a princess to me.'

'I don't know about that,' the princess said, shaking her head before glancing around their humble home. 'Go on then, read to that daughter of yours.'

'Ours, don't you remember?' he said, smiling wickedly.

'Hans Huber.' Maria exhaled with exasperation and then, trying not to smile, added, 'Stop all this nonsense.'

Despite a tough and irritable exterior, Maria had a warm centre, tender and even sensitive, although most people didn't get to see it. People wondered how Hans Huber, a kind and gentle man, tolerated his sullen wife. When Hans wanted to leave a function or meeting early, he said, simply, 'My wife is expecting me home in ten minutes.'

They understood, without further explanation. 'You'd better be going then,' they would say in unison.

Watching her father, it felt like a lifetime since he'd last read to her from the Bible, though it wasn't, it was merely a year prior, the night before she, sixteen-year-old Amelia, had clung to her father's arm like a child of four and begged him not to go. Though he'd served in the First World War, his age and occupation, owning a tailor's shop, it didn't stop him, along with other men of his age, being forced into military service. With the war going badly for Hitler, the old men were rounded up, and after a week's training, sent to fight the advancing Russians. As a soldier, he survived for three months before becoming one of the 30 million to die, casualties of the Eastern Front.

Having finished reading the passage, he closes the Bible and lifts his free hand. Amelia can see he is holding an object, light dancing from its surface. At first, she can't understand what is shining, but as she looks closer, the half of a silver 5 Reichsmark coin pendant that hangs around her neck comes into view.

Amelia's refuge is replaced by a welling of urgency, panic enveloping her. Instinctively, she reaches for her neck, relieved that her amulet is still there, but when she looks back at her father, his hand is empty. Hans Huber smiles and Amelia understands that this isn't her time to die. He lingers for a moment before fading, his soothing smile the last thing she remembers of him.

The absent cold seeps back into her awakening, reluctant, weak body. Involuntarily, Amelia shivers. The peacefulness of the warm tranquil light has been shattered, replaced by a harsh, marred present.

As her eyes open, she observes a city that is now ghostly quiet. The intense sound of roaring flames spurred on by cyclonic howling winds has died away. Moving her head, Amelia looks above her: a ghastly dirty sky is cloaking the city in a shroud, an incarnation of death. A layer of ash is descending to suck away the last remnants of life from any who have had the audacity to survive. She slams her eyes shut, not to be at rest with her father, but as a preparation for the fight for life.

Lying in the gloom, the reality of what has happened slowly returns. Amelia is trapped under rubble, in the bombed and charred ruins of Dresden, a city she calls home. Diffidently, she wiggles her fingers, tries a hand, then an arm, leg, and foot. Nothing appears broken, although her whole body is riddled with pain. Amelia struggles, lifting her right arm, but hits timbers that lie across the top of her body. It is a miracle that she hasn't been crushed and, although unaware, the timbers of the prison are also her saviour, having provided protection from the falling bricks and other rubble. Moving her left arm, the dirt covering it falls free. Wriggling from side to side, she slowly edges forward, but each time, it consumes the little reserves of energy that remain within her weak body. Steadfastly, resting regularly, Amelia struggles on until eventually she is free of her sarcophagus.

Struggling, she attempts to stand, but unsteady on her feet, falls down again. Trying a couple more times,

Amelia gives up and sits instead. Glancing about, Amelia sees she isn't alone. Nearby, only feet from where she has been trapped, are the dead remains of a girl of similar age. A lifeless leg and arm protrude from the bricks and, through the gaps in the rubble, she can see the outline of a corpse. Amelia gasps, shutting her eyes at the awful sight. A cold and powerful hand seems to enter her chest to wrap its icy fingers around her heart, intent on obliterating any remnants of human decency she may possess. Opening her eyes, she doesn't call out or sob, not because of stoic resilience in the face of the grotesque realities of war, but because she's numb. The capacity for empathy lost, or so it seems.

The coin, hanging around her neck, feels heavy as it brushes itself against her skin until she can ignore it no longer. Grasping it, her mind is flooded with the memory of the light and meeting her father. Slowly, Amelia climbs to her feet.

CHAPTER 2

The Ring

Over the centuries I, Guinevere, have witnessed the worst of human barbarity; if anything has changed, it's the ever-increasing capacity of humankind to kill on an industrial scale. By any standard of the time, the aerial bombing campaign over 13 to 15 February 1945 was enormous. The British and American bombers dropped 2,400 tons of high explosives and 1,500 tons of incendiary bombs on Dresden. By the time their task was complete, 25,000 civilians were dead, torn apart, or incinerated in the ancient cathedral city, the capital of the German state of Saxony.

Of those who survived the bombing raid, some wrote of their experience; however, my bearer, Amelia Huber, did not. Instead, I share the words of Lothar

Metzger, which gives some insight to why those days still haunt Amelia's dreams.

It is not possible to describe! Explosion after explosion beyond belief, worse than the blackest nightmare. So many people were horribly burnt and injured. It became more and more difficult to breathe. It was dark. All of us tried to leave this cellar with inconceivable panic. Dead and dying people were trampled upon. Luggage was left or snatched up out of our hands by rescuers. The basket with our twins covered with wet clothes was snatched up out of my mother's hands and we were pushed upstairs by the people behind us. We saw the burning street, the falling ruins and the terrible firestorm. My mother covered us with wet blankets and coats she found in a water tub.

We saw terrible things: cremated adults shrunk to the size of small children, pieces of arms and legs, dead people, whole families burnt to death, burning people ran to and from, burnt coaches filled with civilian refugees, dead rescuers and soldiers, many were calling and looking for their children and families, and fire everywhere, everywhere fire, and all the time the hot wind of the firestorm threw people back into the burning houses they were trying to escape from.

I cannot forget these terrible details. I can never forgive them.

CHAPTER 3

Pendant

This autumn, eight years ago, I, Jacinta Kowalska, moved back from Germany to the UK where, for the previous fifteen years, I was an investigative journalist, to fulfil a similar role for an English newspaper. Also, I wanted to be closer to Mother in her later years, and this influenced my decision to change jobs. Although I was a year past retirement age, I still wasn't ready to stop. Yet, whether I liked it or not, my career was coming to an inevitable close. The newspaper industry had entered a tough new age, with the massive disruption caused by the emergence of social media and internet giants. The likes of Facebook and Google had been diverting advertising revenue away from the traditional media, so newspapers and television networks could no longer afford the salaries of a team of investigative journalists.

While disappointed to be redundant at the end of my latest assignment, part of me was looking forward to the free time, while frightened of how I'd fill the vacuum, especially as work had been my whole life: my husband, family, community and, most importantly, my identity.

***

'Jacinta,' I heard my mother call for the third time.

The previous few weeks had been difficult, even though the day had been drawing closer to when Mother's independence had to be forfeited. Her latest fall had finally sealed the decision. It was almost a year ago to the day since Emma, my mother, had her first tumble, so remaining in the family home for this long had been quite an achievement. At least, that's what I told her. The grim reaper was still distant despite the unsteadiness and the usual array of age-related medical conditions. At eighty-eight, she remained active and definitely "with-it". Mentally alert. The time had come, however, when she needed to be where there was twenty-four-hour care, particularly at night when she became dizzy and disorientated, which caused her anxiety. As the dutiful only child, I had already discussed what would happen when that day arrived. Yet, despite my preparation, leaving her at the care home was a tough moment for both of us. Selfish though this sounds, I was distressed too. But I think it's more than a feeling that you are failing in your responsibilities. It's the reality of your own inevitable mortality that tugs at the consciousness. At least Mother had me but, having never married and with no children of my own, when this time comes, I would be alone. I think it was this thought that made me irritable and impatient with Mother. Secretly, I was frightened. My fate and my mum's fate were intertwined at that moment; stupidly, I felt like I was the only person in the entire world who had to deal with moving a loved one into care. Part of me wanted to run away, hide, stick my head in the sand and make the whole thing go away. But life isn't like that.

Despite what I've just shared, it would be easy to say that putting Mother into care was the reason for a hard couple of weeks, but that wasn't the complete story. Sometimes you read about it in a newspaper, or watch it on one of those reality TV shows, the unveiling of a hidden secret, a skeleton in an ancient closet of a celebrity's family past. It comes as a shock, however, when this exposure involves your own family. Less shock, perhaps, as confusion would be a more apt description.

What little I'd known about my father had been snippets gleaned from a lifetime of a mother reluctant to mention the war. I knew his name was Karl Kowalski, and like my mother, he was Polish. He had been coerced into joining the Wehrmacht during the Second World War and was killed before I was born, but how, where and when, I didn't know. As an investigative journalist, I ought to have tried to unravel his past, but I hadn't, not with any conviction. Once, while researching a German soldier for one of my articles, I searched for my father's military records, but he came back as "unrecorded", which was not unusual, as many records were lost or destroyed in the turmoil of conflict.

I knew I was born in December 1944 in Warsaw, so it said on my birth certificate, and that mother fled Poland shortly after as a refugee, along with thousands of others, to Dresden in Germany. From what I knew of the history, there had been a Polish uprising against the German occupation. It started in August 1944, but was quashed by late autumn. The advancing Red Army had halted on the outskirts of Warsaw before moving in, during January 1945, to what was left of a once lovely city. The city, which had a pre-war population of 1.3 million, was down to 153,000. From my reading, people were frightened of the Russian soldiers with stories of mass murder and rape preceding their arrival. Millions of people, like my mother, fled their advance.

By my reckoning, it was likely Mother was in Dresden during February 1945. If she was still there in late February, probably with me in her arms, somehow she survived the firebombing and the destruction of the city. If those suspicions were correct, then part of me could understand why she kept her secrets. But another part wanted to understand. It yearned to know her story, which was also the beginning of my story.

It seems strange to admit that I knew so little of my heritage and it shamed me. When I was younger, however, I can assure you, it wasn't from the lack of trying. Each time I grilled Mother about her life, the answer was always the same: 'The past is something I've forgotten. England is my home and you're my family.' Over time, I grew to accept her privacy, even though her history was also my ancestry. When I was twenty-four, I wondered if her secrecy was to hide a scandalous teenage pregnancy. When I did the maths, she was forty-six, and thus twenty-two when I was born and, by the law of nature, twenty-one at conception. Considering the period, my parents were of average age when they were wed, especially at a time of conflict.

My mother told me that, because of the war, there were no photographs of my father, the wedding or our extended family. With no memory of grandparents, over the years, I had grown to accept that Mother and I had only each other.

The discovery that was to change my life began the day I took Mother to the care home, when she realised an important personal possession was missing. Uncharacteristically, she had commanded that I return to the family home and search for it. In hindsight, what I found could have been nothing, but maybe unconsciously, I was looking for a new challenge to fill my expected void and so attributed unnecessary meaning to a benign item. But, when I located it and turned it repeatedly in my fingers, I was filled with an overwhelming desire to know Mother's story, even though I knew she wouldn't give it up easily. The Emma Kowalska story was also my story and as I sped towards the autumn of my life, I was determined to understand it. Once I proposed researching the family tree, but it had been dismissed immediately.

From my earliest memories, Mother always wore a chain around her neck, securing a pendant that was rarely seen. If I'd been curious about the pendant, it was so long ago that I no longer remembered.

***

It was the afternoon after her fall, while settling Mother into her new home, the care facility, when suddenly she became distressed.

Grasping her neck, Mother cried out, 'It's gone! Jacinta, it's gone, I've lost it.'

'What's gone, Mother?' I answered dismissively.

'My necklace.'

'I'm sure it will be at your old house. I'll drop by tomorrow and have a look on my way here.'

Sobbing, Mother said, 'That just won't do. Please, Jacinta, go right now and find it... It's all I have.'

She was not set to melodrama, but, given the events of the day, her behaviour was understandable, particularly when most of her possessions had been left behind. There was no space for them in the single room, which was now her home. Although I'd packed some personal items for Mother and, over the next couple of days, would bring additional pieces to add some decoration to her room, we hadn't discussed what was to happen to her house full of "things": furniture, paintings, dining settings, a lifetime of the items needed to make a home, and that were no longer required. To help pay for her care, Mother's house would have to be sold and everything cleaned out.

'Of course, Mother, I'll go right now and have a look,' I told her, rolling my eyes without being seen. 'You needn't concern yourself. I'm sure I'll find it.' Then, demonstrating the little attention I had been paying, said, 'What is it I'm looking for?'

'My necklace, the one I always wear. You're not listening, are you?'

'I am listening, Mother. I was only checking to make sure I got it right. Do you mean the chain you wear around your neck?'

'That's the one. It's my precious necklace. It must have come off when I had the fall. Check the bedroom, on the floor.'

'Yes, Mother.' Looking back at it now, the opportunity was there to ask... *Why is it so precious?* But the thought never entered my mind and I'm embarrassed to confess, instead I was grumbling under my breath, *Can't it bloody wait?*

The drive from the care home in Littlehampton, West Sussex, back to Mother's house in Rustington, where I had grown up, only took fifteen minutes. With no living relatives, Mother immigrated to Britain after the Second World War. She became a teacher at a Church of England primary school, St Margaret's, in the village of Angmering, close to where we lived. The school was one of the oldest in the country, founded by William Older in 1680. She spent her entire career there. An active member of the local church, she never ventured far from Rustington. Perhaps it was growing up in a time of war, but Mother was content in her world, one many would consider closed and narrow.

The three-bedroom bungalow was on a quiet street, a short walk from the church and local shops. Opening the front door, I was greeted by a familiar smell. It's difficult to describe, but for any with aging parents, it's the telltale aroma of an old person. Maybe it comes from them being housebound, the home becoming musty. Whatever it is, there is a fragrance of age, just as, when my friends were having children, their homes held a distinctive scent of babies.

Entering the front door, which opened into the sitting room, I felt compelled to pause and look around. As happened when Mother asked me to search for the pendant, what she called her necklace, I felt a tinge of guilt at my own feelings. Despite this being our family home, I harboured no emotional attachment. Being reminded of the tasks ahead, my first response as I walked towards the main bedroom was to mutter, *How am I going to get rid of all these things? And what a hassle it's going to be to sell this place.*

In the bedroom, while crawling on the floor in search of a pendant I just couldn't seem to find, I cursed aloud in frustration. What should have taken only a couple of minutes was now turning into an arduous task. Starting with the bedside table, I hurriedly swept aside the knick-knacks before opening each drawer and rifling through its contents. 'Nothing,' I muttered in frustration. Next, I rushed to the kitchen, checking the countertops, then moved on to the small living room. Still nothing. Taking a deep breath, I reminded myself, *Slow down. Go back to the bedroom and search meticulously and systematically. Otherwise, Jacinta, you're going to be here all night.*

Getting down on my hands and knees, I hoped to find it under the bed. Again, nothing. I spotted a pair of shoes beside the bedside table. Momentarily dismissing them, I directed my attention to the wardrobe, but then I backtracked and picked up the shoes one at a time. Finally, in the second shoe, I found the pendant, nestled inside as if it had simply fallen there. Grasping its chain, I lifted it from its hiding place, relief washing over me.

In my hand was something totally unexpected, one half of a crudely cut coin. A hole with a punch ring through it connected the coin to a worthless chain. The pendant was so bewildering that my curiosity went into overdrive. Finding my glasses, I studied the coin more closely. It was dated 1936 and had two sets of markings. The first preceded the date and read "Reich". Under what I assumed was the wing of a German eagle were the words "Reich Mark". My annoyance dissipated and, taking out my smartphone, I entered "Reich 1936" into the search engine. A picture of a silver 5 Reichsmark coin appeared. Even though I held only part of it, there was no question. Mother's necklace was half of a Third Reich, Nazi silver 5 Reichsmark coin. My investigative journalism inquisitiveness kicked in and "The Little Grey Cells", as Agatha Christie's Hercule Poirot would say, asked. *Why would Mother wear half a Nazi coin? What gave it such special meaning? Who gave it to her and where was the other half?* I immediately wondered if it was Father.

Perhaps I should have taken the opportunity to search the rest of the house for more clues, but I didn't. I'd like to say it was because I naively believed that Mother would reveal everything when confronted with the coin. However, after the initial excitement faded, I realised that there were more pressing matters to attend to that day.

Driving back to the care home and checking my watch, I realised I was going to miss the appointment with my paper's editor. Annoyed with Mother once more, I phoned and cancelled the meeting.

Mother was relieved to have her necklace back but, when questioned, she reverted to form, dismissing my inquiry with, 'It was during the war,' making it clear the conversation was finished. Maybe it was because I was already feeling annoyed that I kept probing, first gently, then more forcefully.

'Mother, a Third Reich coin! That's an unusual thing to be wearing for all these years. What's its significance?'

Mother didn't answer. Instead, she stared blankly back at me. Although I wondered what was going through her mind, I was determined to show that I expected, no, demanded, an explanation.

'Mother!'

'It's important. Are you happy now?'

This time I would not settle for the emotional blackmail or her avoidance. 'It's important,' I repeated indignantly. 'What does that mean?'

'It's special to me.'

'I know that!'

Mother fell silent. From my training, I knew that asking leading questions when trying to uncover the truth was never ideal; it risked the chance of the person telling me what they thought I wanted to hear. But she was leaving me with no choice. I decided to begin with a proposition that was unlikely to be true, just to see if she would agree with anything I said. 'Did your mother give it to you?'

'Does it matter?'

'Yes, because if it's important to you, it's also important to me. That's all.'

'Your father gave it to me before he died. Are you happy now?' She paused as if that was to be the end of the conversation, but then added, 'I promised him I would always wear it. I don't like talking about or remembering those times. I thought you understood.'

Mother had played the guilt card to win the argument, or in this case, end the discussion. I was having none of it. 'So, he wore the other half?'

'When we were married, we couldn't afford a ring. All we had was this silver coin, which your father cut in two, half for each of us. It's my wedding band and I've worn it faithfully and will continue to wear it until the day I die.'

I wanted to ask her, *Tell me about my father. How was he killed? Where were you married?* But from her stubborn tone, I sensed our conversation was nearing its end. Instead, I said,

'Why a German coin, when you were from Poland?'

'You know, he was conscripted into the German army. That's how he was paid. Please, Jacinta, no more of these silly questions. Britain is our home. Let the past be.'

For the first time, I discovered something personal about Mother, and it surprised me. This distant, impenetrable woman harboured a romantic secret: she had worn one half of a coin, given to her by my father, for the last sixty-six years. The very thought of such devotion and enduring love over a lifetime filled me with wonder. I had to know her story and wondered if there were any other clues hidden throughout the house. If she had preserved this link to the past, there must be others—private treasures that connected to her previous life, unless Mother had already destroyed them. But she hadn't.

It was a couple of days later that I returned to the old family home, this time accompanied by a real-estate agent for a property valuation, and to discuss the sale. I was assured the property wouldn't be on the market long and it would be preferable, for aiding in the sale, if the furniture was left. As we walked from room to room, I found myself constantly distracted by: *How was I going to get rid of all this stuff?* Not only the furniture, but wardrobes of clothes and shoes, no longer needed; the odds and sods; papers, photographs, worthless paintings and the obligatory limited-edition Royal Doulton collectable plates, of which there were many. But another part of me was excited about rummaging through everything, in search of a mystery, perhaps a fantasy of my creation.

When the agent left, and having made a cup of tea, armed with large plastic garbage bags, I made my way to Mother's bedroom to start my search. Decluttering, becoming minimalist, was in vogue and, being a practical person, I decided to clean out as I explored. Items not being kept would go in the bags, one for the tip and the other for the charity shop. Apart from some jewellery, the bedroom held nothing of particular interest or significance, so, with ruthless efficiency, most of it went into the tip bag. Next, I moved to the study. For some strange reason, I enjoyed looking at Mother's old documents, tax returns, bank statements (some twenty years old), school yearbooks from when she was a young teacher, standing next to children now grown up. I put these to one side. Other than a few photographs, a reminder that Mother was once a young, active woman, there were no windows into a life before Britain.

My old bedroom still had the single bed from when I lived there. Other than that, the room was barren. Not even a picture hung on its walls. Mother and I obviously shared the declutter gene. Opening the inbuilt closet, a couple of dresses hung on the racks, overflow from Mother's bedroom. They smelt musty. A suitcase lay neglected in the corner, accompanied by some forgotten footwear. Next to that was an old and battered shoebox; bending down, I removed it. The weight was no surprise, but its contents were. Inside, a collection of old letters, documents and photographs.

My initial excitement was quickly replaced by confusion.

CHAPTER 4

Identity Card

The letters in the shoebox were bundled, tied together by a piece of red ribbon, and finished with a bow. From their appearance, they hadn't been read in a very long time. I picked out the pack and examined the address of the envelope on top. It was handwritten in German script and addressed to an Amelia Huber of Dresden. *Amelia Huber?* I questioned. Untying the bow, I flicked to the next envelope in the sequence, also handwritten. This one was addressed to a person called Peter Kramer, attached to a German army unit. In the mix of seemingly personal letters was an official typed envelope from the German military addressed to Mr Gunter and Mrs Helga Kramer of Dresden. *Were they Peter's parents*? I didn't recognise any of the names. *Why does Mother have these*?

Along with the letters, the shoebox contained three faded black and white photographs. The first, a woman and man with a girl of about three years of age, perhaps a mother, father and daughter. The next was of two children, both about nine or ten years of age, standing side by side, brother and sister possibly. I studied the photo. It seemed this girl was the same as the one in the first photograph. The last picture was of the same children, this time as teenagers, sixteen or seventeen years of age, I estimated. The teenage boy was wearing a Wehrmacht army uniform, so maybe he was eighteen, but he looked younger.

Replacing my find in the shoebox, I carried it to the kitchen and carefully placed it on the table, pulled out a chair to sit and then stared at the contents. My thoughts were a tangle of vines as I reached for the box but withdrew my hand, frightened of the secrets inside. I paused for what seemed an eternity before fingering through the letters an ordered pile in the box. I stopped at the official-looking document. *This is the best place to start*, I muttered to myself and removed the letter from its envelope. Inside was a faded, partly typed and part handwritten certificate, written in German, from the Wehrmacht. The English translation read;

15 Jan 1945

Mr & Mrs Gunter and Helga Kramer

Sternple Street 3 Dresden

H140034 Private Peter Kramer D.O.B. 10 May 1927. I regret to inform you that your son Private Peter Kramer was killed in action, 18 December 1944 Poland. His personal belongings will be made available in due course.

Putting the death notification down and taking the photo from the box, the one of the teenage girl and boy in uniform, I whispered,

Is this a picture of Amelia Huber with Peter Kramer? Who are these people and why does my mother, Emma, have their letters? Unless... is it possible I'm not who I think I am? Could Mother's real name be Amelia? I have so many questions.

Unsettled, I returned my attention to the shoebox and began sifting through its contents, hoping to find more official-looking documents, something to help explain what I was seeing. Nestled snuggly between the letters, hidden but not concealed, was a German identification card. Holding it, a knot formed in my stomach and I hesitated, nervous to open it, unsure of what it might reveal. *Even if it is Amelia Huber's identity card*, I thought, *that does not mean Mother's real name is Amelia.*

Opening the card, I examined the faded, partially damaged picture showing a woman. There was a smudge partially hiding the photograph, but it did not conceal the beauty of the woman staring back at me. Mother had no old photo albums, the war saw to that, and this was the first time I'd seen what was possibly her as a young woman. It was a shock; we have a tendency to view older people as they are now, forgetting that they were once young and had another life.

Moving my eyes from the picture with trepidation, I read the rest of the identity document.

Family Name: Kowalska

Given Name: Emma

Maiden Name: Debska

D.O.B: 04 April 1922

Place of Birth: Warsaw

Nationality: Polish

Kowalska is the feminine of Kowalski and although I felt a sense of relief, as the name on the identity card was Mother's, it raised more questions in my mind.

What was the connection between Amelia Huber and Peter Kramer? Why does she have their personal letters, and what does one half of a silver 5 Reichsmark coin have to do with this?

There was little point in asking Mother, because she would refuse to elaborate. To discover the truth would need the best of my investigative skills, and I had learned over a long career of complex investigations that the suspect is always the last person to interrogate. When armed with the facts, you had a greater ability to know if you were being told the truth or being misled. Until that day, I had largely accepted my mother's reluctance to open up about the past, understanding that her trauma during and immediately after the war was too raw to revisit. Now, I suspected there was another reason, a secret she was content to take with her to the grave. I couldn't let her do that.

Arranging the identity card next to the death notice on the kitchen table, I returned my attention to the photographs. *Who are this boy and girl?* I said to myself. *Brother and sister, or are they Amelia and Peter?* Frowning, staring at the picture of the young man in his German uniform, next to the teenage woman, I suspected they were sweethearts. Placing the photograph next to the identity card, a sequence forming, I compared the picture of the woman with that on the identity document. *Were they the same person?* I thought. Similar facial features and their build were almost identical, but looking closer, the hair was different. Because the identification document photo was slightly smudged, making a direct comparison was impossible. Regardless, after studying each photograph for some time, I felt more or less confident that they depicted different people, even though it would have been easy to mistake the two. The girl in the photographs was likely Amelia, and Emma, my mother, was the subject of the ID card. Countless stories raced around my head as I reluctantly added the photographs and identity card to the shoebox collection and replaced its lid.

I was time to step away from the house and banish the discovery from my mind. But, on the drive home, I couldn't stop ruminating. Eventually, I gave in to it and let my mind settle on a course of action. Using the stamp dates of the envelopes, I would sort the letters into chronological order to help me piece together the tale's timeline. One envelope wasn't postage-stamped and had a handwritten date on it instead. For the first time in many months, I experienced the surge of adrenaline I used to feel when unravelling an important news story. That emotion, however, was quickly replaced by one of emptiness, as I remembered my career was coming to its end.

How would I occupy my free time? I pondered. *Wouldn't it be ironic if my final, substantial piece of investigative journalism turned out to be my story?*

I pushed the thought from my mind and returned to the photographs. Could they hold some clues, recognisable buildings in the background, perhaps a street sign? All would point to the identity of the people in the photos.

Demonstrating an exemplary display of self-discipline, it was two days later before I again examined the contents of the shoebox. Seated at my desk, having date-ordered the envelopes, I took a deep breath before I removed the first letter. It was from Peter Kramer to Amelia Huber of Dresden, Germany.

15 May 1944

Dear Amelia

It's been six long weeks since I left and, although I promised to write every day, I find the constraints of military life make that impossible. I can now understand why the letters, to you, from your father, were infrequent.

At school, I was not as clever as you were, so it's difficult for me to explain and express in a letter how much life has changed. In writing, I want, with all my heart, to be brave like the letters you used to read from your father. After your father left for the front, no matter what we thought war would look like, nothing could prepare me for the reality that awaited.

We were warned that our mail is censored, to check that military secrets aren't exposed, so there's little I can say of the fighting, other than I find myself a man of seventeen wanting to be a boy of six again.

Do you remember when we were six? I was that scruffy kid, new to the neighbourhood, who moved in five doors up from your shop. Before our family had finished unpacking, there you were, banging on the door, keen to welcome the newcomers to the street. We became family, the brother and sister neither of us had. Lying awake last night, I can't recall a day, until I left for the army, that I've not seen you. We walked to school "together", played in the street "together", laughed and cried "together", and got up to all kinds of mischief "together". Almost all of it, I recall was at your initiation. I still remember the time you boosted me through a factory's toilet window, on a mission to steal copper piping from the loo, for the scrap metal man in exchange for an apple each. Do you remember making off with our heist and being chased down the road by the factory guard, dragging the pipe, banging and clattering behind us?

I still dread to think what would have happened if we were caught. Our parents would have banned us from seeing each other for months. We were lucky he was old, overweight and slow, but still, how long did we hide in our secret spot near the river, too petrified to move? Hours. I remember it was pitch black before we were brave enough to walk home while laughing so much that we cried. That was until we realised the time and how much trouble we were in. Unable to see each other for a week as punishment, if memory serves me. Neither of us thought the pipe would still be there when we returned, but as I write, I still remember the delicious taste of those apples and savouring each and every bite. It had been such a long time since either of us had tasted fresh fruit. Thinking about it now, it was the risks we took to get them that made the fruit so sweet. How you convinced me to steal bullets for their copper, I don't know. And then, when the metal man said he wouldn't buy them unless the bullet had been separated from its copper casings, how you convinced me to use a hammer, I'm still at a loss. I always followed you, doing whatever you asked, because you made every day an adventure. I miss you so much and the time we had together. Amelia, I can't stop thinking about you, wondering what it is we would be doing, if I were home. You've always been my friend – my best friend – my only true friend.

My dearest Amelia, many of my fellow soldiers carry photographs of their sweethearts and talk about their dreams for a life together when the war is over and they return safely home. I hesitate to ask, but would you be my sweetheart and send me a photograph to carry and cherish? If you wanted, you could just be my sweetheart until I came home, but I would also understand if you just wanted to remain friends.

Perhaps it's the distance separating us, or the sounds and smells of battle that are compelling me to tell the truth, a secret I've kept to myself for fear of your reply. I think I fell in love with you the very first day, when you banged on our door. In my dreams, I still see Father opening the door and there you are, standing, hands in your pinafore dress with your hair pulled back in a pigtail. Shyly, I looked at you, and with all the confidence that belied your years, you stared back with those beautiful blue eyes and smiled. From that moment, I was smitten, and I always followed one of your escapades, a willing partner. We've played, cried and laughed together for eleven years. Now, wherever I am and I hear a knock on a door, I am taken back to that very first moment.

Dearest Amelia, I end now but will write again soon. I promise never to mention being my sweetheart again unless that is what you want.

I pray your father is safe and your mother is well.

Please take care of yourself and my family until I return. Do try to keep out of trouble, although I would love to hear of your adventures.

Your friend, Peter

When I opened the envelope, I hadn't known what to expect. To my initial delight, I was holding a love letter. Reaching into the shoebox and retrieving the photograph of the young couple, the one with the boy in a German uniform standing next to the woman, I whispered aloud, *Peter and Amelia. It has to be, but why are you here? What's your connection to Mother?* Then it struck me. Rifling through the drawers of my writing desk, I plucked out a magnifying glass. I lifted the photo to look at the girl's neck, expecting to see the Reichsmark pendant. There was nothing. *What's the connection?* I asked myself again before removing the second letter from the shoebox, this one from Amelia to Peter. But I couldn't bring myself to open it, for I knew already that in a few months' time he would be dead. What if Amelia replied, saying she did not love him? I wasn't ready for their story, not yet.

CHAPTER 5

Amelia's Reply

Having kept myself busy by throwing heart and soul into my final work assignment, Amelia and Peter had taken a back seat; not forgotten, but the pressing desire to uncover the truth had settled. Yet a persistent nagging lingered. It felt as though the letters had whispered their secrets to the wind, calling out to me in the stillness of the night. It was three days after reading the first letter, late, gone midnight, with sleep having deserted me. Putting on the bedroom light, I walked to the study, reclaiming the box from its hiding place — the bottom drawer of my desk, where it wasn't a distraction. I retrieved Amelia's reply to Peter's confession of love from the box, but picked it up and put it down twice without opening it. On the first occasion I went to the kitchen and made a cup of tea. The second time, I strolled around the house, wasting time, putting off the moment that I would learn the truth. I'd been unlucky in love myself and found unrequited romance stories unsettling, preferring unlikely fairy tales with happy endings.

I opened the letter; there was no picture inside. Peter had asked for a photograph to cherish, but it wasn't included. *Maybe it's been lost*, I thought.

My dearest Peter. It's with deepest sadness, the letter started – and my heart sank. Was this a "Dear John" letter?

1 June 1944

My dearest Peter.

It's with deepest sadness that I write and share the most tragic of news. Two days ago, although it feels a lifetime, for since then the world has stood still, we received a telegram informing us that Father had been killed on the front line. The next day, any hope we held that the Wehrmacht had made a mistake faded, with the arrival of a personal written letter from his commander containing some of his personal belongings, his wedding ring, watch and wallet. Neither the letter nor telegram said how he died, but the commander's letter said how he had been a respected man among the troops and fought bravely till the end. I'm afraid that I don't find that a comfort.

Mother/Maria is inconsolable, and, Peter, I fear she has lost the will to live. Despite my best coaxing and pleading, I haven't been able to get her to eat since the telegram arrived. She sits in her chair, emotionless, looking at the empty place where most evenings Father would sit, smoke his pipe and read. Peter, I don't know how to help her. Your parents have visited. They tell me to be patient, but I fear the worst. I could lose both of them. Both my parents.

I mustn't burden you with my worries. Hopefully, Mother will find her strength soon. You will be pleased to know that I see your parents every day and they are in good spirits. Times here are still tough and food is in short supply, but we are getting by.

Oh, my darling Peter, you are still at war and I can't bear to think of the horrors you must face, but writing I can only think selfishly of myself. It's unthinkable; what would I do if I lost you as well?

You can't die. I love you and will be waiting for you to return. Peter, I want to spend the rest of my life with you and can't imagine my world without you in it. I know you wanted a photograph of me, but please forgive me for sending one of us together. Do you remember when your father took it? You were in your uniform, just before you left. There's me standing next to you, too shy to hold your hand. I wanted so much to take your hand, but was frightened that you saw me as a sister and not as a woman. I was afraid to touch you, because I didn't want to do something that would scare you away. I was content to be a sister, if that meant I could be with you every day. If only, my darling Peter, I had known your true feelings. That day, as they loaded you and the other men from our home onto those trucks, I would have held you tight, kissed you tenderly on the lips and whispered, 'I love you.' I would have told you I fell in love with you that very first day and secretly, I promised myself that one day you would be my husband. Although, I guess many a young girl thinks that when they are playing mummies and daddies with the neighbour's boy. The difference is, I never forgot. Every day when you came to play, I would say secretly to myself, 'I am going to marry Peter.'

Please, my darling Peter, write back as soon as you can and tell me you will be coming home.

Reading over my letter, I fear I've placed too great a burden on you. All I really want to say is I love you. You mustn't worry about your parents or my mother because they have me to take care of them. Peter, while you are away, if you experience moments of fear or loneliness, know that I'm waiting for you.

My love is your shield, and when this dreadful war is over, for the rest of our lives, we will be together.

I am and will always be your sweetheart. My darling Peter, I love you more than words can say.

Your sweetheart,

Amelia

How quickly emotions change. I was on a roller coaster, at first hesitant, frightened to read should her answer have been negative. Now I was being overwhelmed by thoughts of my empty life without James. I'd not known love in quite the same way that Amelia and Peter were expressing theirs, other than through romance novels, but I had experienced love and lost love. Setting the letter down, my yearning grew – I wanted someone to fill my otherwise mundane and empty existence. Work had been my life, and now it was nearing its end. How wonderful, I thought, it would be to marry your childhood sweetheart. But then the stark realisation took the place of the fairy tale, developing in my mind. A couple of months after Amelia wrote this letter, Peter, like her father, would be dead. Even though I didn't know Amelia and Peter, just thinking about their tragic story caused tears to form in my eyes. It brought back memories of the long-forgotten grief for James, one from over thirty years ago, and I wept uncontrollably. Later, when my emotions had settled, I knew I wanted to write Amelia and Peter's story, even though their time together was short. Looking down at the pile of correspondence, I decided I should not read the next letter until I'd discovered more about each of them. The abstinence would be my motivation to start the research.

It was time for some detective work and uncover the lives of Amelia Huber and Peter Kramer.

The shoebox letters were a promising starting point. They revealed Peter Kramer's Wehrmacht service number, H140034, his date of birth—May 10, 1927—and his parents' address: Sternple Street 3, Dresden, all from the death notification. Identifying Amelia, however, would be more challenging; all I had to go on was her address from Peter's letters. Perhaps Amelia was still alive, and we could talk. If Peter and Amelia's love story was part of Mother's secret—alongside her refusal to discuss the past—unravelling the truth would be difficult without Amelia. Then there was Mother's silver 5 Reichsmark coin necklace. The love letters and the coin could be unrelated; after all, Mother had claimed it was a gift from her husband, Karl Kowalski—my father—before he died. Yet, inexplicably, I felt that the lives of Peter, Amelia, and Mother were intertwined. My working hypothesis was that mother had known Amelia when she was a refugee in Dresden.

Having previously written a piece about German World War II soldiers, I knew that the primary source for historical records on the German armed forces was the Deutsche Dienststelle, part of the German National Archive, or Bundesarchiv. You could submit a written request for information, which is useful if you're a family member seeking specifics. However, for research, a personal visit is far more effective. The National Archives was in the German city of Koblenz. With the advent of the internet, one of the most valuable resources for military information is an online Wehrmacht Militaria Forum. After locating an active forum, I posted an inquiry on their web page.

Hi,

I'm looking for information on a World War Two Wehrmacht army soldier, Private Peter Kramer from Dresden, who was killed in action, 18 December 1944, in Poland.

In my possession, I have some beautiful love letters written between Peter and his childhood sweetheart, Amelia. If someone knew Peter Kramer during the war, or before, it would be a great privilege to hear from you.

Jacinta Kowalska. United Kingdom.

Although it's possible with a computer to do much of your research from home, I've always found that going to the source is more instructive. Having told Mother that I was going to Germany for a couple of days for work, I booked myself on a flight.

CHAPTER 6

Love Letters

My plan had been to go to Koblenz, and the National Archives, but at the last moment I changed my mind and booked a flight to Dresden instead. Here, armed with the details from the correspondence of the shoebox, I would start my search for information on Amelia Huber's and Peter's parents. My hope, church records, such as deaths, marriages and baptisms, weren't all lost in the firestorm and perhaps, someone living in Sternple Street remembered them.

Following my arrival, it didn't take long to discover that the street where the families lived was destroyed during the February 1945 bombing. It was unlikely, therefore, that evidence of the past would be found there. After my initial disappointment, to my delight, I found the Dresden Historical Commission had undertaken a five-year study, reviewing records from the city archives, cemeteries, official registries and courts to determine the actual death toll from the two days of allied bombing. What's more, they had categorically dismissed the rumour that many victims' bodies were never recovered. The obvious place to start then was to uncover whether Amelia, Maria, Gunter or Helga were recorded as killed. Although I doubted that the report sought or could identify individuals, I was praying they'd pulled together the records into a single place. With access to the research and with a little luck, I could determine if they were "known" to be killed. It took only one phone call and the next day I had an appointment with the Dresden Council.

As the initial excitement of discovering the Historical Commission began to wane, I felt a bit deflated. To lift my spirits, I decided to take a walk in search of a place for dinner. After passing twenty charming restaurants, I ultimately chose the hotel's restaurant for its convenience. The energy I had available for new discoveries seemed limited to my love letter search. Back in my room after dinner, with an expensive bottle of red wine for company and acutely aware that I was in the city where the story happened, it was time to tackle another letter.

Nursing a glass of wine, feeling a little melancholy and with the next letter, one from Peter to Amelia, in hand, I settled into a comfortable chair and began reading.

20 June 1944

Amelia, my dearest love,

If only I could be with you, to hold and comfort you, in the news of your father's passing. Growing up together, I know how much you adored your father and that his passing weighs heavily on you and your mother. Be strong, my love. She will need you now, more than ever.

I have been given a few days' leave, so will come straight home to be with you, my love. If the trains are still running, I will be there on Monday 10 July, leaving again on

Sunday. Every waking moment, then in the dreams of my sleep, I am filled with the thoughts of kissing you. I see us kissing passionately and hear myself whisper, 'I love you.' We kiss again, causing my imagination to go wild in erotic expectation. My senses are lost. Your lips are the lips of angels. Then I feel your beautiful body, as it pushes gently against mine. We quiver, as our skin touches, and lose each other in a heavenly embrace.

In my last letter, I said I fell in love with you the very first time I saw you. That's true, but my feelings changed when we were thirteen and our hands briefly brushed together. Although we had touched before, from that moment on, all I could think about was holding your hand. I thought about you differently and became frightened of losing you. From that moment, I loved you not only as a friend, but as a woman.

Even before then, I would have done anything for you – and did. I remember, we had been out on one of your notorious adventures, the ones which inevitably ended in us having to flee. But this one, I think, was the first, where we progressed from childish quests to exploits that could have got us into serious trouble...if we were caught.

You met a man, but never said how, who offered us a chance to sell sausage; not the canned stuff, but real sausage. As payment, if we sold it all, we got to keep some sausage from the next consignment. As I write this letter, I can't help but smile. By thirteen, you had us both working for the black market, though we didn't know it at the time.

I still remember the coat, with the sausage hanging in rows inside. It was too big, so you made me wear it. We were both aware of the danger if we got caught, but at thirteen, we were invincible of course, and didn't weigh up the consequences as we would now. That first day, you bounded off down the street and, like a faithful puppy, I followed along behind, coat and all, with the sausage swinging side to side. At least we went to a part of town where no one knew us.

You approached people passing-by and asked them if they were interested in a purchase. I would hang back, on the lookout for the police and ready to bolt. If they were keen, you would walk them back to me, where I would quickly flash open my coat, exposing the dangling sausage. The boss did warn us, money first, before they got to touch the merchandise.

With three easy sales under our belt and only two sausages left, we became brazen. It was easy money, or sausage, as it was, or so we thought. I can still see him. You should have stuck to the women, because in my mind he looked like an SS officer, although he wasn't wearing a uniform. When he grabbed me, I don't think he was expecting a petite little girl to kick him so violently in the shins, that was all it took for me to break away. We were off, running faster than a red fox fleeing a hunter. I can still hear him yelling, demanding the people stop us. If it hadn't been for your love of sitting on rooftops, he may have seized us when we found ourselves trapped in that dead-end alley. We laughed in fun, or was it fear, as we scampered up that drainpipe? How I managed in that big coat, I still don't know. We ended up, as we always did, in our favourite spot by the river. That's when it happened. Seated next to each other, our hands touched and my feelings changed. I was hopelessly in love and would do anything to remain near you.

You may not remember, but after that adventure, you started complaining that I was bumping into you all the time, and giving you a friendly little shove as we walked together. 'You've become a typical boy,' you would grumble before pushing me back. The truth was, I wanted an excuse to touch you. It was my immature way of showing how I loved you. We boys aren't very clever when it comes to this thing called love.

Oh Amelia, how I long to be with you. Even as the snow falls, when the men about me shiver in cold, the thought of you warms me. I have no fear of war, feel no hunger from the lack of food, or tiredness from no sleep. Nothing compares with the agony of being separated from you. I love you, my gorgeous, wonderful Amelia.

Dream of me, as I dream of you, then our week together will feel like a lifetime.

Darling Amelia, I will be with you soon and, if the trains aren't working, I will walk. Nothing in the entire world, not even the war, will prevent me from seeing you.

I love you with all my heart.

Forever yours, Peter

Wow, I muttered, as I put the letter down, then questioned myself. *Am I being a voyeur, wanting to know what happens next?*

I knew, when Peter returned to Dresden on leave, it would be the first and last time they would meet as sweethearts, because Peter would be killed before he could visit again. I hoped the week was something special and wondered if they made love. Maybe, if they had, it would be mentioned in the next letter. *How horrid of me for wanting to read such a thing.* Then I wondered if they had become engaged. Despite a promise to myself to complete some research before reading the remainder of the letters, I was hooked and needed to know what happened. Rifling through the box, I looked for the next letter, knowing there were two more because I had already seen them. *What!* To my utter disappointment, I found only one. Panicking, I searched my luggage in case it had fallen out. Still nothing. I checked my luggage again before methodically examining the shoebox for a second time. Absolutely nothing. *You can't have lost it!* I called out to no one. Calming myself, I rationalised it had to be at home. It could be nowhere else.

It was my plan to read these "Love letters from Dresden" in chronological order. But because of my stupidity, the next letter, from Amelia to Peter, after his week at home, was missing. The one I had was from Peter to Amelia, hand-dated December 1944, shortly before he was killed. I'd put it away for another day, but then changed my mind.

1 Dec 1944

Amelia, my dearest love.

The fight against the Red Army is going poorly for Germany. The roads are filled with refugees and retreating soldiers. They say that the Russians aren't treating people kindly. It is true my love for I've heard and seen the most unthinkable horrors being brutally committed against women and even children. They are raping all the women. I've never wanted to fight before, but now I fight to protect you and our unborn child.

I wouldn't normally try to frighten you, my darling, but you're having our baby, so I beg you to flee, my love. Should the Russians come to Dresden, our parents may be safe, but not you, my precious. Please think of us and our child. You must leave.

I know you won't want to depart without your mother, but she, like my family, will stubbornly refuse to go. Be brave. Tell them you are with child, our child. Implore them to come with you for the sake of their future grandchild, but if they refuse, you must go.

The officers say Germany will win, but we are an army of old men and children. If the authorities are telling you the same, don't believe them. Germany is defeated and the Red Army is intent on making us pay. Some of the older soldiers say the British and Americans are racing the Russians to be first to Berlin. Despite the danger, you must join the race and find the British. They say, of all the troops, the British are the most disciplined, but if not the British, then the Americans. I know I'm sending you towards the eye of the storm, but you can't be caught in land held only by the Russians.

Take the money I've been sending and use it for the journey. Travel by train while you can, there is enough to pay the rent when you reach Berlin, until I join you.

You must go because I'm fighting with all of my ability to give you time to escape. If I were to die, don't let my death be in vain. My soul would weep if I thought you were not safe.

Write to me from your new home, so I can find you when this horrid war ends. We will be together as a family. Our lives will start anew and, God willing, our sons or daughters will never endure such difficult times.

Last night, I dreamed again of the first time we made love. When you met me at the railway station, even though we had been writing and declared our love for each other, the entire trip to Dresden I'd been worrying about how to greet you. Could I hug or even kiss you, or should I just say, 'Hello'? Do you remember? When I saw you, I started to run towards you, but then froze a couple of metres away, staring at you hopelessly. 'You're a funny man,' you said, laughing, throwing your arms around me and kissing me on the lips. I was so intent on wrapping my arms about you, I totally forgot about the suitcase I was carrying, hitting you in the middle of the back with it. I knew the first thing we had to do was visit my parents and then your mother, but the whole time we shared with them, I could think of nothing else but being alone with you. That first day and night, there was no time for us, I couldn't leave my parents, who were so pleased to have me home and even though I went to bed in the house of my loved ones, I couldn't help feeling lonelier than I'd ever felt before. Lying awake that night, I feared that, even when we were together the next day, there would be no place for us to be alone.

I can't describe how happy I was when the next morning I heard that familiar knocking on the door. You took me by the hand and we wandered through the streets as we had done as children, which was only months before. Laughing, we told of our adventures together, but really, all I wanted was to kiss you and say, 'I love you.'

It was on the steps of the Church of Our Lady when I could resist the temptation no more. Still holding your hand, I stopped, pulling you to a halt. You turned and faced me. I flicked a wisp of hair away that was hanging over your eye, then stroked your cheek with the back of my hand. Your face was soft and tender. Slowly lowering my hands to rest on your shoulders, I pulled you towards me. I knew there was no one else about and we were alone on the steps, but other people weren't on your mind. You came to me and we had our first true lover's' kiss. I remember stepping back and admiring your beauty, silhouetted against the backdrop of the church. I knew you were my angel from heaven. Looking into your eyes, I said, 'Amelia, I want to be with you for the rest of my life.' You smiled and mouthed without speaking, 'Yes.' With my heart spinning, you led me away. 'Where are we going?' I asked. 'You'll see,' was all you would say. The moment you took me towards the river, I knew that you were taking me to our secret hiding place.

You pulled me down on the ground to be next to you and we kissed like never before. Both of us were overwhelmed by a desire to be together, to be joined as one. I see myself slowly undressing you with you smiling as each layer was removed.

In your underwear, I started to remove my shirt, but you stopped me, pushing my hands to my side. 'I want to do it,' you whispered, then gently removed my top and trousers. Taking my hands, you placed them on your breasts and I could feel the warmth of your skin, as I ran my hands around your breasts, finding the nipples. You smiled, and I traced the outline of your body, moving towards your legs. My fingers caught the top of your panties and slowly I removed them to reveal your womanhood. I kissed you again, taking in and savouring the sweet smell of your fragrance. You removed my underpants, then, as you lay on your back, you pulled me with you, guiding me inside. As we joined, you sighed longingly, saying, 'I love you, Peter,' and we made love.

The truth of war, my love, is there are moments of intense fighting when you hold on to life by the lightest of touches. The combat is then broken by long intervals of nothing, and that's when the cold and fear eats away at the remnants of courage you are desperately holding onto. It's the thoughts of you, my love, the memory of that moment near the river that keeps my mind and heart from falling into the abyss.

Before I leave you in this letter, I beg you once more, fly, my angel, with our child. Write to me when you are safe and I will come.

A friend of mine, John, is travelling to Dresden and has promised to carry this letter with him. With God's will, it should find you quickly.

I love you with all my heart.

Forever yours, Peter

Pouring another glass of red, I took a large gulp then whispered, *She's pregnant! Don't die, please don't die.* Closing my eyes, I prayed she fled Dresden before the allied bombing. Drifting off to sleep, I had a vivid dream re-enacting the romance and meeting Amelia with her child. As my eyes drifted open, the fantasy ended, the realisation of why I came to Dresden flooding my mind. My hunch. Mother met Amelia in Dresden, in February 1945. If that assumption was true, she hadn't been able to escape, as Peter had pleaded. Knowing that Amelia had been pregnant, I now, more than ever, hoped she wasn't one of the confirmed victims. Desperately, I longed for a happier ending to this romantic tragedy.

The next morning, armed with the letters and other documents from the shoebox, I met one of the historians, Karen Fest, who worked on the Dresden study. My first inclination was to tell a small fib that I was a relative of Amelia from the letters. I thought a family connection might boost my chances of looking at the Dresden records, but when I met Karen, I felt compelled to tell her the truth.

'It wasn't feasible for us to determine, with any degree of certainty, each individual person who was killed during the bombing,' said Karen. 'The report rather sought to determine the number of deaths from the aerial campaign. Despite popular belief that the remains of many victims were not found, we determined this not to be true.'

Despite hearing the news I was expecting, it was still disappointing. Even if I was given access to all the raw data, it would be a long and painstaking exercise to discover whether Amelia, her mother and Peter's family were killed, and even then, it may not be conclusive. For a moment, I drifted off and Karen's voice droned in the background of my ruminations.

'Electronic database.'

'Sorry, Karen,' I said, my focus returning to her talking. 'Did you say, electronic database?'

'That's right, cemetery records from both in and out of Dresden, files from local courts, and any official record pertaining to the bombing were put into an electronic database. Over 60,000 records. This allowed us to cross reference, with several records often found for the same person. We gathered data for both the identified and unidentified remains.'

'The people I'm looking for, if they were identified as being deceased after the raid, their names would be in the database?'

'That's right,' said Karen. 'However, many were never identified. We believe we know the number of people killed, but not who they all were.'

'Would it be possible to run my list of names through the electronic database, on the off chance they are recorded?'

'Sure. If you give them to me, I'll do it now.'

With an anxious knot of anticipation in my stomach, I handed over the names I had already written out on a piece of paper:

Amelia Huber

Maria Huber

Gunter Kramer

Helga Kramer

Reading from the paper, I watched as Karen entered the first name. She spoke as she typed so I could follow what was happening. 'Amelia Huber. Now all I do is click on the search key.' She pushed the button. After a brief pause, she said, 'We have a match. Do you have an address?'

With my heart racing, I handed her one envelope with the address written on it. She looked at the envelope and then the screen, before saying, 'I'm really sorry, but she is confirmed as deceased'.

'Thank you,' I said and although I didn't know Amelia, it didn't stop the tears from forming. Karen handed me a tissue. 'Would you mind trying the others?' I asked. They all came back the same, "confirmed deceased". The families, Peter and Amelia, along with their unborn child, had all been swept away by the ravages of war, leaving me with a lingering sense of bitterness and emptiness. My quest was at its end. There was no point in searching for Peter's military records because he was dead – what more could they tell me? The last remaining avenue was to ask my mother, and I suspected I knew the outcome. 'I can't recollect where I got the letters from,' she would say. Or perhaps, 'They were some people I met a long time ago, but they are all gone now and I don't want to remember.' The mystery, Mother's, would remain as she wanted it. Unspoken.

CHAPTER 7

Dresden, World War Two

After the death of her husband, Maria Huber acted out the motions of living. Cooking, eating and sleeping, but she was dead inside. The first night the bombers came, Amelia had pleaded for her to seek shelter; she refused. Frantic at the sounds of plans, Amelia ran to Gunter and Helga Kramer, Peter's parents, who lived in a small three-room flat above a shop, five doors up from their store. She'd begged them to come and convince Maria to go to a bomb shelter. They came but, because they understood Maria's feelings, having lost their son Peter on the Eastern Front, rather than encouraging Maria to leave, they stayed with her.

'Please!' Amelia had begged in tears to all of them. 'Come now, before it's too late.'

'What will be is the will of God,' Maria had said as she smiled.

Between February 13 and 15, 1945, Dresden endured four devastating bombing raids. After the first night of bombardment, during the brief lull before the daytime raids began, Amelia returned home to find her mother's house reduced to rubble.

***

The coin, hanging around her neck, feels heavy as it brushes itself against her skin until she can ignore it no longer. Grasping it, her mind is flooded with the memory of the light and meeting her father. Slowly, Amelia climbs to her feet.

The devastation awaiting Amelia as she stood amid the rubble should have been overwhelming. The city stretched out before her, utterly destroyed, but she felt numb. Gradually, the world around her sharpened, and she heard the sounds of people searching for survivors. Desperate, Amelia cried out, "Mother!" But the only response was silence; she was alone. Feeling the baby move, she clutched her pregnant belly. For a moment, she feared something was wrong because she had months yet to run. As she looked at her tummy, her eyes caught sight of the small overnight bag poking from the rubble near where she'd been trapped. It contained her few treasured possessions, letters, photos, identity documents, things that were irreplaceable. With her eyes half closed in despair, she shuffled across and pulled the bag free. Some of its contents spilled and, in her dazed state, she pushed them back inside and walked away. Amelia had no sense of time, unaware of how long she'd been unconscious. Confused, unsure if she'd wandered into a different part of the city, a city now difficult to recognise, Amelia was enveloped by a hive of activity. Near a statue, standing tall, indignant, in the rubble, men were piling up the bodies of those who had perished during the raid. Incomprehensibly, Amelia was drawn to the sight and standing in silence, she watched as another corpse was added to the growing pile. The traumatic scene causing her to withdraw further inside of herself.

After seeing the piling bodies, Amelia had sunk into despair and, with her home, family and lover having each been lost to war, there was nothing left in Dresden but the fear of the advancing Red Army. Unconsciously, she numbly joined a caravan of fleeing refugees. Some were heading for Frankfurt, others to Nuremberg, and a few, like her, were making the journey to Berlin. But where the caravan was heading was of no consequence. Amelia joined the ant trail of people on the road, yet, unlike her fellow insects, she had no sense of time or purpose.

With war raging, it seemed all of Poland and much of Germany were on the move. People escaping only to flee once more.

***

'*Biegać, Lauf* – run!' Amelia in her distant state didn't hear the screams from a woman, not more than a couple of years older than herself, initially in Polish and then in German, though they were directed at her. The first she knew was the feel of a firm hand pulling at her.

In a detached state, Amelia observed a woman holding a toddler in one arm and tugging at her with the other. The woman was distressed and Amelia was awash with confusion. The past two days had been a blur, and now the world was suddenly coming back into focus. If Amelia had longed for the sweet sound of chirping birds and the gentle rustling of leaves being blown in the breeze to greet her, it was not to be. Instead, she was awakened to the unmistakable buzz of dive bombers and the sounds of deadly explosions coming closer. The woman with the child pulled at Amelia again, before running to the edge of the road and flinging herself into a ditch. Amelia followed and, moments later, the dull light of the last days of winter detonated into scorching brightness and booming sound, bringing with it what war does best: death. As quickly as the outburst of intense violence had arrived, it was over and the crusade to escape resumed. Amelia and the woman climbed back onto the road.

'Go on, grab it,' came the voice of the woman as Amelia stared at a pram abandoned by the death of its owners. Seeing another bounty hunter approaching, the woman thrust her baby towards Amelia. 'Take her,' she demanded, pressing her child into the startled arms of Amelia. 'Piss off,' the woman cried with venom, while shoving a much older lady away from the lonely pram. Holding the woman's child, Amelia took in her surrounds. Watching, she saw those who had survived the attack acting like hungry vultures, picking over the possessions of those who hadn't. The inhuman spectacle was over within a couple of minutes. Anything of value had been picked clean. Those grieving the loss of a loved one were lifted to their feet by strangers to continue their journey into the unknown.

'Take it,' said the woman, pushing the pram towards Amelia while holding her arms out to take her child back.

'It's not mine!' That's what Amelia wanted to answer, but she couldn't. When was the last time she had eaten, washed, or even slept? She couldn't recall because everything was a blur. Then she remembered the haunting sight of the pile of dead bodies in Dresden, biting her bottom lip and with a private sniffle of grief, forced herself to regain focus.

Motioning towards the pram, the woman commanded, 'Go on then, look inside. See what you've won yourself. Mind you, if it's food, you have to share, and any money. That's the deal.'

'What if it's a baby?'

The woman scoffed. 'A baby! Don't be ridiculous. They wouldn't have left a child in the pram when they scarpered from those bombers.' Tentatively, Amelia looked inside the old and rickety pram, peering under its torn black hood. Inside was a dirty pillow with a loose-fitting blanket covering the base. Pulling back the blanket revealed eight cans of food, four packets of biscuits and a large red tin, inside of which was a dark brown-black fruit cake. The owner, she thought, must have been saving the fruit cake for a rainy day, as it was untouched. Tucked in the corner of the pram lay a battered document case, sealed tightly with a zipper.

'Ooh... Not bad pickings,' said the woman, looking over her shoulder. 'We are going to have a nice old feed tonight. Go on then, see if there's any money.'

Cautiously, handling the document case as if it was about to explode, Amelia undid the zipper, revealing two identity cards. An old man and woman, husband and wife, in their late sixties, from Poland. Along with the identity documents were personal papers and, considering the circumstances, a healthy stash of cash. 'Hand it over,' said the woman, looking at the money. Amelia passed the money to the woman and, as her eyes were being drawn back to the identity documents, they were snatched away from her.

'That's not a good idea,' she said to Amelia. 'Best not to know who they were, otherwise it can weigh on the conscience.' Checking the document case for anything else of value and finding nothing, she put the identity cards back inside, closed the zipper, and flung it away. Then, after stuffing the money into the pillow and putting her infant in the pram, she snapped, 'Let's go,' and strolled off in front of Amelia. She stopped briefly and looked back towards where Amelia remained motionless, letting her eyes drop to Amelia's pregnant belly. 'Do you want your baby to die?' she called back coldly.

Amelia shook her head.

'Then keep up.'

Together they joined the trail of people who were heading away from one war front to find another. A safer one, if there were such a thing, away from the Russians.

For the first time since the bombing of Dresden, Amelia realised she was cold and began shivering. The surrounding fields were covered in a blanket of snow and, unlike other people on the road, she wasn't wearing a warm coat, only a jumper over a dress. The chill of the last days of winter penetrated and shook her bones. With a light sprinkling of snow beginning to fall, Amelia muttered aloud, 'I'm cold.' Her travelling companion, hearing Amelia speak, looked towards her and noticed she was shaking.

'You poor thing,' she said, without intended malice or criticism, knowing that many people had been forced to flee with nothing but the clothes on their back. 'We've got to find you a warm coat or you'll not see the end of the cold nights.' She remembered seeing an old man in their caravan, maybe in his eighties, pulling a cart, on top of which sat a German soldier's woollen trench coat. Stopping, the woman searched for the man and, while blocking the road, the lifeless souls following walked round them without saying a word. 'There he is,' she said aloud, but to herself. At the end of the procession, only just keeping pace with the wandering pack, was the old man. Head down, looking at his feet, he edged slowly forward, pulling a cart with wobbly wheels.

If the man was startled when the lady with the pram spoke to him, he didn't show it. 'Hey. How much for the coat?' she said, pointing to the top of the cart.

The squeaking cartwheels came to a slumbering stop. Lifting his weary eyes to meet her gaze, he said, 'Well, young lady, a very good afternoon to you.' Then, looking towards Amelia, added, 'And your friend. How may Artōrius be of help to you?' He gave a slight and courteous bow.

'Good afternoon – *Guten Tag*,' said Amelia, managing a smile despite the cold. She liked the old man immediately and fought an urge to curtsy.

'Your friend. She's German,' he said in a strong Polish accent to the woman pushing the pram.

'A German woman feels the chill as we do, but this one has no coat to keep the frost from her bones. Look closely. See, she is with child.' Maintaining her eye contact with Artōrius, her expression softened. 'We would like to buy, for the right price, the soldier's coat on your cart. Or we could trade? When was the last time you had fruit cake?' Reaching into the pram, she removed the red tin, lifted its lid and displayed the contents.

At the mention of food, the old man instinctively licked his lips. Like so many on the road, he was constantly hungry and hadn't eaten in a day and a half.

He had been waiting to reach the next town, where he hoped to trade some of the items he'd accumulated along his travels for his night's dinner. 'What else do you have to eat?' His statement sounded harsh and greedy to ears that wanted to protect their supplies, although his question was genuine. Artōrius wouldn't take the last morsels from the young women. He'd witnessed too much cruelty over the last few years and feared losing his own humanity in a battle to stay alive. Many had succumbed to their resident evil.

'Don't be greedy, old man,' snarled the woman. 'Look about you. Everybody else has gone. It's a fair trade or else I'll just take it, along with everything else in your cart. You will be another body on the road, missed by no one.'

'It's true,' Artōrius replied warmly while looking at Amelia, who couldn't hide her horror of her fellow refugee's threatening statement. 'I wouldn't be missed. They are all gone.' After a brief pause, he looked back at the woman with the pram. ''My wife, my children and grandchildren. All dead. Maybe it's for the best if you killed me. It's what I deserve, because I couldn't protect my family.' There were no tears, just sadness in his voice. His words tore at the woman's conscience. 'If it's God's will that I die here, then I welcome it, but, child, to take a person's life in cold blood is a burden. A heavy load, and I feel a great weight already travels with you.' After another moment of silence, he continued, this time talking to Amelia. 'Give me your hand, child.' He reached towards her. She wanted to resist but couldn't, stretching to meet his touch. Artōrius's hands were rough and worn, savaged by a lifetime of hard work, as was his contoured and furrowed face. His shoulder-length, snow-white hair and well-cropped matching beard complemented his weathered features and were befitting a man of the ages. Amelia felt strangely safe and wondered whether they'd met before, but dismissed the thought as her imagination.

Holding Amelia's hand in his, Artōrius whispered, 'You're cold, my child.' And then, exploring her features with his beaten eyes, added, 'You remind me of my granddaughter, Davina. She would have been seventeen today. It's her birthday. You both have the same hair and those knowing blue eyes. It's your caring smile that reminds me of her the most.' Letting go of Amelia's hand, he bent down and lifted the woollen coat from the cart, giving it to her. 'It's a gift from an old man, but promise me you will live well. There's already been too much anger and hatred.' Before Amelia could thank him, Artōrius picked up the handle of his rickety cart, lowered his head, and shuffled forward. Wearing her new coat, Amelia and the woman pushing her baby in the pram fell in behind him. After a few paces, they drew up alongside and walked together.

'We are having a banquet tonight,' said the woman with the baby. 'Would you do us the honour of joining us?'

He turned his head slightly, angling it towards her voice. 'Ah, fruit cake?'

'Better, "Keks Świąteczny", Polish Christmas cake, and we also have some dry biscuits.' She smiled.

'Keks Świąteczny,' repeated Artōrius. 'I have some Krupnik. That's vodka with a little honey and herb added, which I've been keeping in case of an injury. It makes a wonderful disinfectant. There's enough for a small glass each and is just the thing for a banquet, and to warm you on a frosty night.' He lowered his head and trudged on. No one said so, but they had become a travelling group of three, four if the baby was counted.

The two women slowed and allowed Artōrius to walk a few paces in front. 'I'm Emma,' said the woman pushing the pram and then, pointing towards the baby, added, ''Jacinta.''

The other lady replied, 'Amelia.'

'Where are you heading?' asked Emma.

'Berlin.'

'Me too.'

Introductions completed, they walked the next half hour in silence, deliberately shortening their strides to avoid overtaking the old man. Although it was only mid-afternoon, the winter daylight was fading. In the distance, they saw the beginnings of a medium-sized town, and the tail end of the human caravan they'd been travelling with was entering its city limits.

Emma looked at Amelia and, speaking loud enough for Artōrius to hear, said, 'We'll have to find a place for the night in that town. We've probably enough money to rent a room, but I think we should look for a railway station or an old hall to sleep in, save our Pfennigs for another time. We may even be able to purchase something hot to eat, if it's cheap enough.' Nobody replied, but a plan for the night had been set.

CHAPTER 8

Town

If the fleeing refugees had hoped the aerial bombing and its destruction were confined to the larger cities, they were to be disappointed. Entering the town, they could see that buildings recently destroyed were smouldering and rescue personnel were combing collapsed sites in search of survivors or undetonated ordnance. The emergency team stopped working to look at the trio, pulling a cart and pushing a pram as they slowly made their way past them. With so many refugees on the move, many towns had opened halls or communal buildings for temporary shelter, as people transited. But tonight, many of the townsfolk were themselves in need of a roof, so Emma wondered how they and the rest of the caravan would be viewed. The people they had met on their journey hadn't been cruel but, when a tipping point is reached, when the number of displaced people on the move becomes overwhelming to the local population, or their own plight is equally desperate, solace becomes scarce.

A little further up the road, in an area that had escaped the carnage, they came across a corner store.

'I'll see if I can buy supplies,' said Emma to the others. 'And some milk for the baby.' In the hope it may encourage the store owner to sell to her, Emma carried the child in with her. The bell atop the door dinged as she entered. An older, solidly built woman came out from the back to the serving counter. As well as holding baby Jacinta, Emma clutched some of the cash they'd found, so the shop owner would understand they weren't begging.

Attempting to convey a hint of warmth despite her sombre expression, Emma said, 'Guten Abend— good evening. I would like to buy a little milk for the hungry baby and a few tins of food for myself.'

The woman responded in a flat and dismissive tone: 'You will need special milk from the pharmacist for the baby.' Without waiting for a reply, she continued: 'Do you have your rationing coupons?'

Emma shook her head, before saying, 'I lost them on the road. It's been a long journey.'

'Then I'm afraid you will have to go to the police and get new ones issued.'

'I can pay,' pleaded Emma. 'What about some bread? That's not rationed.'

'I'm sorry, but that won't be possible. We have scarcely enough food for those living here. I must keep what we have for the townsfolk. You would have seen we've been bombed ourselves. For weeks, hundreds of people have been coming. At first, we tried to help, but there are just too many of you. Try to understand,' she said with no emotion. 'I want to help, but I cannot. We have so little left that our babies and children are going hungry, too. Every one of you who comes in here holding a small child wants a small amount. These add up. It breaks my heart, but I have to say... No, so please, leave. There's nothing for you here. All the shops will tell you the same thing.' The detached woman then folded her arms and stiffened her frame, a sentinel guarding her treasure.

Many thoughts and responses flooded through Emma's mind, some of them not charitable. Emma held her tongue and said, 'I understand your dilemma and the pain you must feel unable to feed starving children. I bid you a *Gute Nacht* – good night.' As Emma turned to leave, the woman failed to notice her scan the shelves behind and the rest of the shop, remembering where things were stored, in case she visited again, after closing hours. Emma knew, however, if she broke in and was caught, it would be the firing squad. What choice did Emma have? Without food or milk, her child, Jacinta, would die.

Outside, she reunited with Amelia, who was waiting. While talking, Emma noted the location of the windows and laneway running beside the premises. Not wanting to draw attention to herself, fully aware that the shopkeeper was watching, she lifted her gaze to the second story where the owners would have lived. A window next to a drainpipe was slightly ajar—*a possible entry point*, she thought. Amelia seemed to read her mind, sensing exactly what she was considering.

While Emma was in the shop, the old man, Artōrius, had gone scouting for shelter for the night. A little further down the road, he found a derelict building, damaged in a previous bombing raid, which offered some shelter. He estimated eleven other people had already made it their home, and he saw they'd started a small fire from material found scattered about the site.

'Did you find anything?' asked Amelia when the old man joined them back at the shop. He nodded before saying, 'It's not much and others have already claimed part of it. When I spoke to them, I counted ten, but there's plenty of room. It will offer shelter from the cold. They said they were waiting for a train leaving in the morning for Brandenburg, it's not far from there to Berlin. Maybe we could try to board?'

'I know this will sound pitiless,' said Emma, 'particularly if they've offered to share their roof, but I think we should eat our rations before we go. It will save the embarrassment of not wanting to share. People are getting desperate and I've seen folk killed for their supplies, even a warm coat. You can't be too careful.'

'Wouldn't we want people to share with us if we had run out of food?' asked Artōrius.

'Yes, but they wouldn't,' answered Emma bluntly.

'You may speak the truth, but does that mean we, too, must drop our humanity? It seems mean of spirit.'

'Before we go, let's cut a slice of cake each and put it together with a couple of dry biscuits,' suggested Emma, ignoring Artōrius's words. The woman in the shop had been spot on, she thought. Charity begins at home. 'Then we hide the rest of our provisions. If we have to share, it's only tonight's rations that are at risk.'

'If you wish,' answered Artōrius.

'I'm sorry,' Emma continued, 'but I have more pressing troubles. I need to find milk and something for Jacinta to eat. I haven't been producing enough breast milk and have resorted to giving her sugary water.' Taking a deep breath to fight back tears, she added, 'Baby Jacinta is so weak now that she's even stopped crying from hunger. If I can't trade my share of our supplies for milk, I'll have to resort to stealing something. I'm not being selfish by not wanting to share; it's Jacinta that I'm thinking of.'

'Have you stolen before?' asked Artōrius warily.

'No.'

'I have,' said Amelia. Then, glancing towards the shop, added, 'Even pregnant, I could be up that drain in a second. Like a rat up a sewer pipe.'

'This way,' interrupted Artōrius, picking up the timeworn handle of his trolley, left in the care of Amelia while he went exploring, and started walking towards their lodgings, with the cake tin remaining unopened in the pram. Dusk had given way to a moonlit evening and with no cloud cover, the temperature would plunge. It was also an ideal night for a bombing raid. In the distance, they could see the glow of fire coming from within the abandoned building, their home for the night. Ordinarily, the authorities would have demanded the fire be extinguished, to provide no targets for planes above. Tonight, with remnants of fires still burning all over the town from previous attacks, their small fire was too insignificant to earn the wrath of the Reichsluftschutzbund (RLB) – National Air Raid Protection League.

'Welcome,' said one of the women huddled around the fire. Although she was wearing a tattered overcoat with a scarf pulled tightly over her head, hiding her facial features, Amelia guessed she was in her fifties. Away from the fire, Amelia spotted the silhouettes of two children playing. The scene was more reminiscent of a gypsy camp than a gathering of displaced people. Above the fire swung a black steel pot swung from a tripod.

'Well, come on in then,' said the woman, seeing the trio were hesitant. Then, looking towards the pram, asked, 'You have a child?'

'I have a baby,' answered Emma with all the confidence she could muster, although she was feeling intimidated.

'What of you?' continued the woman looking towards Amelia, who shook her head.

'Come into the light, where I can get a better look at both of you.' Amelia, Emma and the old man joined the gathering. The woman, who hadn't taken her eyes off Amelia, said, 'You're with child, yes?' Amelia wondered how she could tell, when her pregnant belly was hidden under the coat.

The woman took the lid off the black pot and stirred its contents. 'Have you eaten?'

'We have some cake and biscuits,' proffered Emma.

The woman nodded, and for the first time, a little tenderness crept into her voice. Glancing at Emma, she said, 'What about the baby?'

Emma, struggling to hold back her tears, couldn't speak immediately, then said, 'I can't feed her. I've tried, but I haven't any milk and no one will sell us any.'

Since meeting Emma, only hours before, Amelia believed she was the lost and frightened child, while Emma was the self-reliant, worldly woman. The truth surfaced. Emma was troubled and scared, just as she was; they both clung to life with a feeble grip.

'Boy or girl?' asked the woman.

'Her name's Jacinta,' answered Emma.

'Let me see her.' The woman put down her stirring spoon and held out her arms to take the child. Emma passed Jacinta without hesitation because she radiated a mystical presence, making her command compelling. With the baby in her arms and looking at the child, she said. 'Hello Jacinta, they call me Lena.' Lifting her eyes, she added. 'We haven't got much more than flavoured water with an elusive potato and cabbage leaf floating in it for soup, but it's warm. Sit down, all of you, and share our humble meal.'

'Thank you,' sniffled Emma. 'I will give my portion to Jacinta.'

'You're a silly young thing,' grumbled Lena while handing Emma's baby to another lady who was sitting next to her. 'You can't take care of a child if you're starving. Leave Jacinta to us. Basia will look after her tonight.'

The woman holding the baby looked up and smiled at the mention of her name and then said, 'Don't worry yourself, I'll make her a little something, this evening she will go to sleep on a full belly.' Basia looked into Jacinta's eyes, started humming softly and rocked her tenderly back and forth, then smiled at Emma before catching the gaze of Lena. In that second, as they exchanged glances, Basia's eyes told Lena that it would be God who decided the fate of that tender baby tonight. The infant's life was as delicate as an autumn leaf blowing in the breeze. Her fortune rested with a greater power.

'I can take care of her,' said Emma, not wanting to appear helpless after Lena's reprimand. 'Your most kind, but you needn't worry yourselves about us. After tonight, Jacinta will be alright.'

'Indeed,' answered Lena, gesturing again for them to be seated. 'You can tell us about your plans after we have shared tonight's blessings.'

One of the other people seated around the fire, a woman, wearing old socks over her hands, with the ends cut out for fingers and thumbs, passed Artōrius, Amelia and Emma a bowl each. Lena stood and, after lifting the lid from the pot, ladled the watery soup into the company's bowls. Each person received one and a half scoops, except for the newcomers, who were given two. Having completed the full circle and before feeding herself, the pot was empty. Picking up her bowl, Lena served herself the imaginary broth, remaining standing to eat so that no one was aware of her generosity.

Artōrius placed his meal in front of him and went to his trolley, retrieving a tin of dry crackers, which he handed round the circle. No one spoke as they ate, instead enjoying the warmth of the liquid as it radiated from the bowls to thaw their cold hands, then heated their insides as they swallowed it away. There was little taste, but that didn't matter, it was food. Afterwards, the people around the fire introduced themselves. Unlike Emma, Amelia and the old man, who were unexpected travelling companions, the others knew each other before they had fled. Lena, the woman who had welcomed them and served the meal, was the unofficial leader.

'Tell me,' Lena asked Emma, 'what are your plans?'

Emma immediately regretted her stray words because informers were everywhere. But after a momentary hesitation, she dismissed the idea that any of these women were working for the SS or Gestapo. Anyway, part of her needed to say she had a scheme, so as not to appear a naïve and helpless child.

'There's a small general store back up the road,' started Emma. 'I was thinking of visiting it in the early hours of the morning and taking a little milk and a few cans of food. Just enough to feed Jacinta and nothing, you understand, for myself. I intend leaving the money, so it's only kind of stealing, out of desperation. We asked the shopkeeper, but they wouldn't sell us anything.'

'I see,' said Lena as she pondered Emma's revelation. 'Have you considered what would happen to baby Jacinta if you get caught? You know they will probably shoot you, and at best, you could end up in jail.' Before Emma could answer, she turned to Artōrius and asked, 'What do you think of this idea?'

He thought for a moment. 'These are extraordinary times and mothers have to go to extraordinary lengths to protect their family. I wish it were that I was younger, for I would do it myself, but if this is what Emma needs to do, then I will go with her.'

'Me too,' pronounced Amelia.

'No,' came a gruff rebuke from the old man. 'If something were to happen to Emma, then baby Jacinta's future rests with you.' As he was speaking, the air raid sirens began to wail. The old man stood. 'Now's the best time,' he said to Emma. Then, speaking to Amelia and the women seated around the fire, 'if we're seen, we won't come back here. Look for us at the railway station in the morning. Come,' he said, reaching his hand towards Emma, who took it to help her stand. Emma looked at Basia, who was still holding and gently rocking her baby.

'Don't worry, if anything happens, I will take care of her,' said Amelia, seeing concern written across her face.

As they left their bombed-out fortress, Lena called after them, 'There's a curfew, keep out of sight and don't get shot. Godspeed.'

Although the night remained clear, some shards of cloud had formed and, when they passed in front of the bright moon, the lights seemed to be turned down. Carefully, they made their way towards the shop with Artōrius in the lead, keeping to the shadows, hugging the buildings, darting in and out of doorways. Emma was surprised by how easily he moved, as it was at odds with his shuffling gait along the road, dragging the trolley precariously behind him. The old man stopped, raising his hand, telling her to halt. Emma could hear the sounds of people chatting. Straining her eyes, she searched for them.

'Back,' Artōrius whispered, guiding her into an alleyway they had just passed. It was darker than the road they had travelled, but they would still be visible if anybody glanced in their direction. 'Here,' she heard the old man say, before feeling his hand pushing her hard up against a side entrance to one of the buildings.

The air raid sirens had long since fallen into silence, and the stillness of the evening now felt like the calm before a storm. The old man nervously listened. He was anxious and, although the approaching people had stopped speaking, he could hear the sound of their steps as they strode the footpath. When they reached the alleyway, the footsteps fell silent. Emma and Artōrius pushed themselves further into the wall. Thirty seconds passed when Emma was tempted to peek, to see if the foes had gone. The old man, having sensed her impatience, held her against the wall. Moments later, they heard steps hurrying away, heading down the road.

The two stayed in their hiding place for a minute before deciding it was safe to leave. They heard the drone of bomber engines in the distance. It was too late to seek shelter. Life or death was now like a black or red spin of a roulette wheel. 'Come on,' the old man whispered.

When they reached the shop, somewhere off in the night, the first bombs were falling. The whistling noise made by the ordnance as they tumbled to earth couldn't be heard at their distance from the target, but the sound from the massive explosions as they detonated on impact seemed as if they were only feet away. They could break a window to gain entry; the sound of shattering glass would likely be lost amidst the chaos of the night. But unless other windows in the shop or nearby buildings were also shattered by the bombing raid, a forced entry would have invited the police to search for looters in the morning, something to be avoided. It was best to slip in and out like ghosts, leaving little sign of their incursion. Once inside, Emma planned to take only what she needed to sustain her child, which she hoped would go unnoticed by the owners until they fled the city. The upstairs window was still slightly ajar.

The next explosions, to Emma's fright, were closer, heading in their direction, one detonating only a little way up the street. Its thunderous boom was ear-piercing and, despite the chill of the night, the gush of wind that followed carried with it the heat from the blast. Having been in Dresden during the firestorm, Emma panicked, primed to take flight; to where, it didn't matter. The old man was unruffled. He touched her reassuringly on the shoulder and gave a calming smile. It settled her as if by magic. Artōrius pointed to the drainpipe and said, 'Up you go.' As he spoke, there was the sound of another eruption, but this time it was further away. 'Be quick,' he encouraged. 'We won't have long.'

Emma surprised herself with how easily she scurried up the drainpipe, then, holding on with one hand, reached over, pushed up the window and slid in through the curtains, before carefully pulling the window back down. Although it was dark inside, with her eyes already adjusted to the shadowy light, Emma could just make out the obstacles in her path and navigated her way out the bedroom, down the stairs and into the shop. Quickly, she made her way to where she remembered seeing cans on the shelves. Reaching up, she grabbed a couple. The light was too poor to read the labels, but she took them anyway, putting them on the counter, while looking for the milk. It was then that she saw it, a cardboard box without a lid. Inside was a bottle of milk, a loaf of bread, and four cans of food. Emma surmised that the cheerless shopkeeper had guessed her desperate thoughts. She felt humbled by the tenderness and generosity of a woman she didn't know and ashamed of her own dishonesty. In place of the box, Emma left money and then hurried out the front door to the sounds of exploding bombs.

'She's a strong one,' said Basia, while handing baby Jacinta back to Emma, after they safely returned from their clandestine shopping mission. 'We must water down the milk because it's a little rich for one so young,' she continued. 'Comfort your child while I prepare its bottle. Then, my dear, after feeding Jacinta, you must rest. We have a big day ahead of us with a train leaving in the morning.'

The morning brought another clear, wintry day. *At least it isn't snowing*, thought Amelia, as she accepted a bowl of porridge from the ladies with whom they'd shared the fire.

After eating, Lena, the leader of the women, declared, 'It's time to leave for the railway station,' and looked expectantly at Emma, Artōrius and Amelia to see if they were going to join them.

The old man and Amelia stood ready to go, but Emma reluctantly shook her head. 'Baby Jacinta has a fever,' she whispered. 'I can't leave until she's better.'

Basia, using the back of her hand, touched the child's forehead and nodded in agreement, saying, 'She's running a temperature, but a train carriage may be a warmer place for a baby than here.'

'I'm sorry, but I can't leave,' repeated Emma firmly. 'Not until the fever passes. You go on without me,' she said, looking at Amelia and Artōrius.

The old man smiled. 'This constantly getting up and sitting down is not good for one's back.' He lowered himself down again. 'What would I do with my trolley on the train? They would make me leave it behind and all I have left in the world travels in the cart with me. I'll stay, and besides, we're travelling companions.'

'And I've lost all my identity documents,' Amelia confessed. 'It must have happened after the bombing of Dresden. I woke up trapped under the rubble, and since I never go anywhere without them, they must still be there. All I know for certain is that they're gone—my identity card, ancestor passbook, ration books, and clothing books. If the SS or police catch me, they could throw me in jail, or worse, assume I'm a Jew and take me away. Trains aren't a safe place for me at the moment. Best I keep away from such things until I get my papers replaced, maybe in Berlin. I also stay.'

Lena, in a reprimanding tone, said, 'These are dangerous times to be travelling without papers. It would have been best to replace them in Dresden, where you were known and before venturing away.'

Amelia lowered her head. 'I know,' she replied. 'I remember waking up after the air raid and seeing men piling up bodies, then nothing until yesterday when I found my new friends. I didn't even realise the papers were missing until last night. Now I'm frightened. I know what happens if you don't carry them.' She sat down.

The old man touched her kindly on the arm, saying, 'Oh, don't worry yourself, my dear, I know just the person in Berlin who can remedy that for you. I'll take you to see him as soon as we arrive. In the meantime, if we are stopped, all you have to do is tell the truth. The miracle of telling the truth is you don't have to remember what you said. You might be questioned, but you will know the answers. Any SS officer worth his salt would know that you are telling the truth. As well, you have Artōrius and Emma to protect you. We are all staying,' he said to Lena.

'As you wish. Be safe, my friends,' said Lena as she and the other women left.

For the next four days, they lived in the bombed-out building. There were no more air raids, but they could often hear the planes flying overhead, en route to some other unfortunate town or city. Jacinta's fever broke on day three, but they waited another twenty-four hours to be sure the baby was well enough to travel.

The sounds of footsteps moving through the rubble hadn't concerned them, because Artōrius had left earlier in search of supplies for the next part of their journey. Emma and Amelia both jumped, however, when from behind them, an unfamiliar male spoke. 'Good morning, *Frau*.'

Turning, they were confronted by two uniformed SS officers. One, an older man in his mid-fifties and the other, a younger person, perhaps in his twenties. Neither woman spoke, both frozen with fear. Emma was cradling her baby.

The older SS officer spoke again, maintaining his soft demeanour. 'Where are you going?'

'Berlin,' answered Emma, then quickly averted her eyes away from him to look at her baby.

'Why are you going to Berlin?' the younger man demanded, his tone unpleasant and contrasting sharply with that of his companion.

Lifting her eyes again, Emma answered, 'The Russians are coming.'

'Where have you come from?' asked the older officer, looking at Amelia, who had not yet spoken.

'I left Dresden after the bombing. My family was all killed. I just ran.'

The officer nodded knowingly before looking at Emma.

'Warsaw,' she said.

'Papers, Pol,' instructed the young man aggressively. Emma struggled to hide her shaking and fumbled for her identity documents while holding Jacinta before regaining her composure. Handing them over, she met his eyes, saying without words, *I'm a woman with nothing to hide*.

'Are there any more of you?' asked the older officer.

'I'm travelling with them,' said Artōrius, who had returned without being noticed, moving to stand beside Amelia and Emma.

They ignored him, and while holding Emma's papers in one hand, the younger officer reached toward Amelia, indicating that he demanded to inspect her documents. 'I've lost them,' she replied timidly.

The young SS officer looked at his companion, who said kindly, 'What's your name?'

'Amelia, Amelia Huber.'

'*Frau* Huber, may I inquire, where did you lose your papers?'

Amelia rambled, with stress and fear colouring her speech. 'In Dresden, it must have been after the bombing. My mother was killed in the raid, my father died fighting with the German army, I just ran, you see... I don't even know how it happened. Maybe I dropped them. In Dresden.'

'You're lying,' snapped the young officer, grabbing her by the arm and yanking her towards him.

His SS colleague saw rage building in the old man's eyes and lifted his hand ever so slightly, signalling to Artōrius that he should remain calm, before saying, 'That's most unfortunate, *Frau* Huber, I'm sure you understand we must take you with us, while we confirm your tragic story. Some people we meet are not as honest as you appear. They don't always tell the truth. It is a matter of routine.'

Amelia stopped struggling in the hold of the young SS officer, and he lessened his grip. Without her papers being checked, the SS officer thrust them back to Emma. Artōrius was not asked for his papers.

'I have personal letters... with my name on them,' Amelia pleaded. 'They will prove who I am. They're in the pram, from my fiancé—he was in the Wehrmacht, the army.'

The SS officers ignored her pleading, instead started marching her away.

'Excuse me,' called Artōrius politely, but with purpose, after them. 'Where, may I ask, are you taking her?'

'To our headquarters,' snarled the younger officer, who gave Amelia an aggressive tug at the inconvenience of having to answer a question.

'Could I come with her?' asked Artōrius to the more mature of the SS officers.

Before he could reply, the younger man said, 'Only if you want to be thrown in the cells with her.'

'You needn't be worrying yourselves,' interjected the SS officer's companion. 'I'm sure this will all be cleared up quickly; *Frau* Huber will be back with you by this evening. We are only taking her to the local police station to make the necessary inquiries. Just routine, I assure you, in these cases when someone has lost their papers.'

In an instant, Amelia was gone, bundled into the back of a waiting car and driven swiftly away. Emma, her baby and the old man were left alone in the bombed-out ruins, feeling helpless.

'We'll never see her again,' said Emma, with a tone of inevitability decorating her voice.

'The world moves in mysterious ways, my child. Now is the time for patience,' came a reply lathered with quiet resolve.

Emma started rocking Jacinta, then looked to Artōrius, and said, 'I haven't asked where you're from. That seems so rude of me. I'm sorry.'

'I'm a traveller. There's no place I call home but where I rest each day.'

'What about family?'

'Friends like you are my only family now. Others have long since passed.'

***

'You're hurting me,' complained Amelia, being led from the car towards the police station with the young SS officer gripping her arm tightly.

'Otto,' said the older officer, '*Frau* Huber isn't going to run away. I think we can let her walk on her own.'

Otto let go of her arm, but not before squeezing it as hard as he could, causing Amelia to yelp. He smiled in perverse satisfaction.

Once inside, Amelia was taken to a bleak interview room, windowless and starkly furnished with three chairs and a table. The only adornment was a picture of Hitler, which hung on the wall. Amelia was seated in the chair opposite the two SS officers, who were now armed with pen and paper. 'If we might go over this again.' The older officer smiled. 'Your name?'

'Amelia Huber.'

'Date of birth?'

'3 May 1929.'

'Address?'

'Sternple Street 13, Dresden.'

'How do you spell, Sternple?'

It felt to Amelia as though the interrogation had been ongoing for hours. They wanted to know where she was on this day, then another. The names of her parents, her grandparents and even their parents. Who was the father of the child and where had he lived? Early in the questioning, after Amelia had repeated her personal details, Otto, the younger SS officer, had left the room, returning a couple of minutes later.

Although Otto didn't ask many questions, he would constantly interrupt Amelia's answers with an abrasive, 'You're lying... Now tell us the truth.'

'I'm telling you the truth,' Amelia would plead. 'Why won't you believe me?'

The older SS officer looked at her sympathetically. 'We want to believe you but, with no identification papers and the fact that you can't tell us where you have been since the bombing, this makes it difficult. We have been searching for a German woman about your age, same build, hair colour and height. This woman is a traitor, an agent working for the Americans. They call her the "Crimson Tiger", she's been responsible for–' A knock interrupted him mid-sentence. A police officer handed Otto a piece of paper, which he read before passing it to his colleague. After looking at it, he said, 'I will ask you one more time. What's your name?'

'I've answered that,' wept Amelia. 'Amelia Huber.'

'You're lying,' snapped the younger SS man, slapping Amelia hard across the face as he spoke. Her head was knocked sideways by the impact of the blow. 'Amelia Huber was killed in the Dresden bombing; her body and papers have been recovered. You see, we know you're lying. You are a Jew or a spy. Which one is it?'

'Think carefully before you answer,' cautioned the older officer in his conciliatory tone. 'Jews, we deport, spies, we shoot. I want to help you, I really do, but the choice is yours.'

Weeping uncontrollably, Amelia begged to be believed. 'I am Amelia Huber, a German woman from Dresden.' Ignoring her pleas of innocence, she was forcibly taken from the interview room and dumped into the cold and damp of a dark prison cell. Her toilet was a bucket in the corner of the room, and her bedding, a tattered old blanket, barely thick enough to ward off a mild chill, let alone the biting cold of early spring. Sitting alone in the dim light cast from a single globe hanging from the ceiling, Amelia finally stopped sobbing. *What does it matter? All the people I love are already dead*, she thought, then, feeling the baby move, the awfulness of her situation flooded in. *If only they would take me to Dresden, someone would recognise me and then they would know I'm telling the truth*, she cried to herself.

In the chaos, the final days before the inevitable collapse of Germany, she realised her life meant nothing to these brutal men; they would probably enjoy butchering her before the killing of war stopped. Amelia knew the SS were murderous, lawless thugs, and vowed not to cower before them, or give them the pleasure of hearing her plead for her life. Her death, she was determined, would give them no satisfaction.

Surviving the cold and on meagre rations, only barely enough to stave off starvation, Amelia languished in the cell for a week before the older SS officer retrieved her.

'Come,' he said.

She wanted to ask where they were taking her, but said nothing. Instead, she pumped out her chest and, standing tall in resolute defiance, followed behind him. Outside, Otto, the younger SS officer, was waiting by the car. He opened the rear door, and she got in. He then sat beside her. The older man climbed into the driver's seat, started the car, and they drove away. As they manoeuvred their way through the streets, nobody spoke. They left the town limits and headed out along a country road. Shortly, they turned right onto another country lane, which led into a forest. This road was deserted. They drove for another ten minutes before pulling the car to the side of the road and stopping. Amelia's heart was racing.

'Get out,' said the driver. As he spoke, Otto, the SS officer sitting beside her, opened his door and stepped from the car. He moved round to stand next to Amelia's door. 'Get out,' repeated the older SS officer.

Giving her hair a calm, nonchalant flick by quickly moving her head to one side, she opened the door and stood beside the car.

With his pistol drawn and pointing at her, Otto commanded, 'Move,' and then gestured with the gun toward the forest. Amelia started walking, and he fell in behind. Every few steps, she felt the barrel of the gun being pushed into the middle of her back. When her foot caught under a fallen branch, it caused Amelia to stumble. As she fell, her arm was grabbed violently by the SS man behind, dragging her back onto her feet. Standing beside her, Otto gave her arm a violent yank, causing her to yell out in pain.

'Keep looking straight ahead and don't speak,' he whispered, while giving her arm another aggressive tug. 'When you hear the gunfire, fall forward onto your face and lie perfectly still. Don't move, don't breathe, and do nothing until we are gone. I've told your friends where to find you, so wait here and don't come back to town. Kneel,' he commanded loud and aggressively. She hesitated, so Otto pushed Amelia onto her knees and then moved to stand behind her.

Amelia's mind and heart were racing, not knowing what to believe.

Is this a ruse to make me complicit in my death?

She was certain of one thing: she would not live.

BANG!

Amelia gasped. She felt the bullet spin past her ear and then saw a spit of dirt fly up as it struck the ground in front of her. Frozen, her mouth fell open. A foot in the centre of her back gently nudged her forward. She allowed her body to fall face first into the leaves and stayed motionless, waiting for the sound of retreating footsteps. How long she remained too frightened to move, Amelia couldn't tell. If the car had left, she hadn't heard it go. An eternity later, Amelia raised herself to her knees, alive and, other than a few bruises, hungry and cold, she was unharmed. Making her way back to the road, she looked in both directions and saw nothing. *Don't be stupid*, she growled at herself for breaking cover, so moved back into the surrounding foliage to wait for her friends, if Otto could be believed. Even if he had lied, she was too shaken from the ordeal to travel far.

'You look cold,' came the now familiar voice of Artōrius. She turned and saw the old man's face, an angel from heaven come to protect her. Amelia wanted to speak but was too overwhelmed with relief to find adequate words.

'Did they keep that wonderful coat I gave you?' Not expecting a reply, Artōrius kept talking. 'Most uncharitable of them, but I have another, and it's just your size. Well, it would be if you were a little taller, but it will fit snuggly over that growing tummy of yours.' Artōrius started taking off his jacket.

'That wouldn't be fair,' exclaimed Amelia, putting her hand up, indicating that he should stop taking his coat off. 'It's yours. I can't take it from you.'

'Nonsense, look, see, there's another one underneath.' Smiling, he attempted a little humour to reassure her, as he continued removing the coat. 'Artōrius has more than he needs to stay warm, that is, as long as you don't mind sharing his fleas.' He held the removed coat towards her. Amelia hesitated. 'Let me help you.' Holding the coat open, Artōrius stepped behind her, slipping it over her shoulders and then said, 'Now that's better.'

Amelia immediately felt the warmth ripple through her body and any hesitation she harboured for taking it dissipated. Putting her arms in the sleeves, she pulled it tightly around her. Artōrius, momentarily shivered but hid his discomfort.

'Did they hurt you?' he asked.

Amelia shook her head and, finding her voice, asked, 'How did you find me?'

'That abrasive young SS officer, he told us where they were going to take you. He also said we were to keep out of sight until they were gone and then wait some more. Which is precisely what we did. Emma and the baby are here too. Jacinta is in your pram. All in all... given the difficult circumstances, I say we're in good shape. And we are together.'

'The SS officer. Did he say anything? Like, why he was helping.'

'No, just where to find you and left. We came here last night and camped under the stars, just to be sure we weren't seen. Kindness sometimes comes from the most unexpected quarters.'

'I'm hungry,' said Amelia.

'I have just the thing for that. Come on, follow me. Emma's going to be pleased. You had us both worried.' Realising that in trying to make Amelia feel safe, he may have inadvertently trivialised her experience, he added, 'But probably not as worried as you have undoubtedly been. You're safe now, Amelia. We are all back together.'

CHAPTER 9

Lost Love

What now? I thought. Having allowed myself four days in Dresden, there seemed little point in staying, now that I knew Amelia had died in 1945. My plan had been, after Dresden, to travel to Koblenz and the National Archives to find Peter Kramer's war records, but that now also seemed pointless. What more was there to know? He died in 1944. I begrudgingly accepted that the story of how my mother came to have the love letters was to remain a mystery.

After the bombing, much of Dresden was rebuilt to its original state and, having nothing else to fill the rest of the day, I decided to walk to the street where Amelia and Peter had once lived as children. There was something inherently soulful about staring at number 13 Sternple Street, believing that Amelia and her mother had all perished there during the war. A shiver passed down my spine, as if they knew I was there. The Huber family had come to an end just like mine when I pass. With no children, the Kowalskas will join the Hubers and be lost to time. In the end, we all become memories.

It's not that I didn't want to have children, but circumstances conspired against it happening. And, while standing outside Peter's old home, 3 Sternple Street, a few doors down from Amelia's, the memories of James became hauntingly clear.

I was a young twenty-eight-year-old, quite beautiful, or so Mother would say, and more interested in travel and career than men, marriage or children. While working, I was staying in a B&B, in the quaint English village of Tiding Springs, to interview a reclusive author who lived there.

My daily routine was to wake early, a little after six o'clock, have a brisk walk, something I did when at home or away. I would then find a nice café, preferably with an outdoor seating area, to enjoy a mug of coffee while reading the morning newspaper.

Tiding Springs had a wonderful park, open and green, established trees, mostly deciduous, typically English with oaks, sycamores, ash and limes predominant, and a walking track meandering its way through them. I noticed the man approaching, spotting first a sprightly golden retriever walking a few steps in front of him and to his side. The dog would continually snatch a look backwards, making sure his master was keeping up. It looked cute and brought a smile to my face, which I quickly hid, not wanting the man to think I was smiling at him as we passed. I refocused my attention on "eyes front" and remembering rule number one, no eye contact with strange men.

We were only a few feet away from passing by when the goldie broke rank and veered into my path, causing me to stop abruptly, before nuzzling my hand for a pat.

'Fitz,' called the dog's owner. 'I'm terribly sorry, he never does that, he's so well-behaved. Fitz, come here.' But the dog ignored the call, giving my hand another gentle push with its head, as if saying, 'I'm so cute, give me another pat.'

'It's OK, I love golden retrievers. Who's a beautiful boy, then?' I said, as I gave Fitz a vigorous rub, the dog looking up, panting, its tongue hanging out.

'Truly, he's much better behaved. He's never done this before.'

I laughed. 'Is this what you tell all the women, that your highly trained, but cute, dog stops for you?'

The man looked back, horrified at the suggestion. My humour was falling flat. His demeanour suggested that all he wanted to do was flee, fearing he was going to be accused of wrongdoing.

'Fitz, here now!' he commanded in a stern tone.

'Who's a beautiful boy,' I repeated, still stroking him furiously while trying to think of a way to recover from my impromptu comment. 'Have you had him long?' was the best I could manage.

'Since he was a pup.'

The man smiled while answering the question, perhaps realising my stupid comment was not meant to be accusatory, but flirting. *Flirting, was I really flirting?*

Politely excusing himself, he started walking away, calling to the dog as he left. 'Come, Fitz.' The dog gave me his look of exasperation, as if to say, 'I tried,' before trotting off, tail wagging, after his master.

The rest of the walk was uneventful, although I discovered something about Tiding Springs, so different from large cities. It was obligatory to exchange a warm 'Good morning' when passing a fellow walker, which, after an initial hesitation, I found quite heartening.

After buying a newspaper, I found a quaint café with outside seating, allowing me to read while enjoying my morning coffee, oblivious to the world. A furry creature knocked my leg, which hit the table, causing my cup to splash its contents, forming a sticky river that flowed across my paper. Fitz's head pushed against my thigh, glanced back to its master as if to say, 'Look, see who I've found.'

'I'm terribly sorry,' came the man's voice behind me. 'I don't know what's wrong with him this morning.'

I turned.

'Oh, it's you again, the lady from the park. How terribly embarrassing. He's not normally like this at all. Please let me buy you another coffee.'

By chance, the waiter popped out of the door and, seeing the man, said, 'Good morning, James and Fitz. Can I get you your normal?'

'Please, and...' he said, looking at me.

'A flat white, extra hot,' I said.

'Do you mind if I join you?' asked James.

'Please,' I answered, pointing to the vacant chair, holding out my hand and saying, 'Jacinta.'

'James, and you've already met Fitz. I think he likes you.'

For the next two mornings, we met at the park and walked together before having coffee at the same café, after which we went our separate ways for the day. The third morning was my last day and night in Tiding Springs before leaving for home. As we walked together in the park, my mind drifted, wondering if he would ask me to accompany him for dinner, a farewell meal, perhaps? When he didn't, I ruminated that he probably had a girlfriend, or a wife, and couldn't be seen with me. *That's silly*, I reprimanded myself, *because he's meeting you at his regular café, where he's known!*

'I'm leaving tomorrow,' I said as we drained the last remains of coffee from our cups at the café, even though I had told him this before.

'I know, Fitz and I will miss our walking companion.'

My heart started to race as I contemplated what I was going to do next. *Anyway*, I said to myself, *what's the worst that could happen?*

'Would you like to have dinner with me tonight, before I go?' Now my heart was really pounding, which seems funny thinking about it all these years later, because I was a grown woman, behaving like a lost teenager.

'That would be lovely,' he answered, smiling, surprised, as if he'd won the lottery. Then, patting and looking at Fitz repeated his words, 'That would be lovely, wouldn't it?'

We spent a wonderful evening together and knowing so little about each other, there were hundreds of things to talk about. The restaurant had switched off the air conditioning, started vacuuming the floor and stacking the chairs as a signal that it was time for us to leave, but we were both desperate to hold on to the moment.

Walking me home, he asked, 'Will I see you again?'

'Would you like to?'

'Very much,' he said.

That was the beginning of one of the most wonderful two and a half years of my life. For Fitz, it may have been love at first sight but, for James and I, our love grew, blossoming as we spent more time together. We didn't move in with each other because of our work commitments in different parts of England. We never missed a weekend together, and we always made those moments special. The distance between us during the week only heightened our desire to reunite, creating a deeper longing that made our time together all the more precious. Each Friday night, our relationship was renewed with passion as fresh and exciting as the first time. I would want to grab hold of him the moment he walked through the door, feeling him close to me and want to rip his clothes off and make passionate love. But James always wanted to savour the moment. He would hold me, running his hands over my face, telling me how beautiful I was before he undressed me tenderly, kissing all the bits as my body was revealed to him. If we fought, I can't remember. My memories of our love are as intense as any fairy tale.

For my thirtieth birthday, James took me to Paris, the city of love, for a romantic dinner for two on the Eiffel Tower, overlooking the glittering city lights. Between courses we held hands and I remember clinking our champagne glasses and sipping the wine, staring lovingly into each other's eyes. James put his glass down, reached into his pocket, removing a jewellery box. Opening and pushing it towards me, I saw a gleaming engagement ring. He whispered, 'Will you marry me?'

'Yes,' I cried. 'Yes.'

We decided there was little point in having a long engagement, choosing instead to be married six months later. James, an engineer, thought it wouldn't be difficult for him to find a new job, so we decided that, after we were married, he would move into my place, before we bought a house together.

We never missed spending a weekend together—until after our engagement. At first, the changes were subtle, but they soon became more pronounced. The first shift I noticed was in his mood; the once fiery passion of our love began to dim. When I asked him if something was wrong, he would deflect my concerns with excuses or apologies. 'I'm just a little tired,' he'd say, or, 'This damn headache just won't leave me alone.'

One Friday night, I waited up to past midnight, expecting him to arrive, but he didn't show. Eventually, I rang at one thirty in the morning, worried that there had been a car accident. He answered the phone sounding groggy from sleep, muttering, 'Oh gracious, I'm so sorry, honey, I thought I would close my eyes for a bit before driving down and I must have drifted off. I'll leave first thing in the morning.'

I confided to one of my friends who told me she thought he was living a double life, possibly with another woman. The thought of another woman in James's life tortured me. When he was absent, my stomach churned, emotions seething with jealousy. I found it difficult to concentrate, wanting to drive to him for a surprise visit, but more to spy than surprise. The reality, I was petrified of what I might discover. All the while, the clock was ticking towards our wedding day.

When it happened again, another Friday evening that he didn't show, that was the last straw. No more excuses. I wanted, no, needed, to know the truth, irrespective of the consequences. As the clock struck midnight, my car raced towards Tiding Springs. I pulled up outside the house. The bedroom light was on and a car parked in the driveway was not James's. My emotions mingled, anxiety, anger, grief, despair. I couldn't bear to discover what I didn't want to find, so I drove off, to stop again, a few blocks down the road. *You have to go in;* I shouted to myself. *Be brave.*

Parking on the street, so as not to be heard, I carefully placed my key in the lock, opening the door as quietly as I could. I wanted nobody to be aware of my presence. The house was in total silence, but the upstairs bedroom door was open, streaming out light, making it just possible to see my way. Under the weight of my footsteps, the floor creaked loudly as I tried to stealthily approach the bedroom. No one stirred. Peering around the door, to my utter relief, James was alone in the bed with Fitz laying at the foot. He opened his eyes, looked at me, but didn't stir. Suddenly, I felt utterly ashamed of my suspicions. Gently, I leaned over and kissed James's forehead tenderly. 'Hi, my sweet,' I whispered, hoping he'd wake up.

James opened his eyes, but they stared vacantly back, before showing signs of recognition. He smiled and said, 'Jaaa...cinta.' His speech was slurred, and I panicked.

'James, James, are you OK? Speak to me.'

'Jaaa...cin...ta,' he slurred again. I rang for an ambulance.

At first, the emergency department thought James had had a stroke, but that was ruled out after a few tests. Over the next couple of days, he had further investigations until we were given the news that everybody fears. James was diagnosed with brain cancer. The headaches, mood swings, fatigue, forgetfulness, they'd all been warning signs, ignored by both of us. Worse, rather than seeing the man I loved was ill, I had interpreted the symptoms as evidence of infidelity. I felt wretched from the prognosis and my guilt. The specialist told us he could have brain surgery and chemotherapy, but the outlook was not good. The intervention, they said, could worsen his quality of life and was unlikely to prolong it. In the end, James chose to forgo treatment, but we decided to proceed with the wedding, though James was expected to live only a few months. He never made it. With Fitz and me at his side, James passed away a week before our wedding day.

After that, I buried myself in my career and then left England altogether, moving to Germany for the first of three times. Love wasn't to find me again. As for Fitz, he lived a long and happy life with my Mother.

Remembering my brief life with James, I wondered if this journey to Dresden was a search for the ideal romance, the one that had escaped me. Why did all the beautiful stories end in tragedy? I dismissed my melancholy, declaring that it was time to move on from my obsession with the love affairs of people I had never known and who, in all likelihood, had been lost to the shadows of earlier, darker, decades. Next morning, I boarded a plane and returned home. The shoebox of stories could gather dust in my cupboard, as it had done in Mother's house. As Mother would say, it was time to put the past to rest.

CHAPTER 10

Emma

They shared what little food they had and, for the first time in days, being warmer and safe, Amelia started feeling better. Though it had been just over an hour since she had escaped certain death, her thoughts shifted to reaching Berlin. 'We should get going,' she said sharply.

'It would be wise to stay off the road, at least for a few days, maybe longer,' recommended Artōrius. 'My suggestion. Once clear of this forest, we should take a cross-country route. Until then, we're forced to follow this road. If we hear a car or anyone approaching, take cover in the trees until they pass. We can ill afford to take any risks.'

'What about the pram and your trolley?' asked Emma. 'We may be able to drag them over the fields, but crossing the fences and ditches with them would be impossible.'

Artōrius thought for a moment, then, ever so slightly tilting his head to one side, said, 'You have a suggestion?'

Emma sighed. 'I could make a sling for Jacinta and carry her on my back like before the pram. There's no food left anyway, so we carry what possessions we can and the rest gets left behind.'

An hour later, they set off and even though the first part of the journey was by road; they decided to leave the trolley and pram hidden in the undergrowth.

After two and a half hours of walking, they finally cleared the forest and, except when they threw themselves in a ditch, mistaking the sound of an approaching plane for a car, they saw no one and went unnoticed. Exiting the wood, they left the road, heading across farmland, and although they knew they might be

162

seen, thought it unlikely they would be recognised or inadvertently run into the SS officers.

The sky hung heavy with moisture, finally unleashing a torrential downpour. Rain, driven by a biting cold wind, whipped around them. Within minutes, they were drenched. Emma did her best to shield baby Jacinta from the chill and damp, but it was impossible to keep her completely protected. Silence enveloped them as they trudged onward, each aware that finding shelter was no longer a priority, but a necessity. Artōrius, leading the way, turned and nodded toward a row of trees in the distance to their right.

'There,' he said, pointing. Amelia and Emma could see nothing except a line of trees. Before they could reply, Artōrius had dropped his head to shield his face from the rain blowing towards him, altered course, and was striding out in the new direction. It took another thirty minutes of hard walking before they reached the treeline where, through the branches, they saw a stately manor, as it was called in Britain, a chateau in France. If either Emma or Amelia wondered how Artōrius knew the whereabouts of this house, the grandeur of it quickly pushed the thought from their minds. A German flag was flying on a flagpole at the front of the residence.

'Come on,' said Artōrius.

'Won't it be occupied?' questioned Amelia.

Artōrius pulled at his white beard thoughtfully, before saying, 'I would conjecture that it was used as a German officers' retreat, yes, that would be it for sure. With the war almost over and the Russians coming, I'm confident they have fled. It should be quite safe for a few nights and, with any luck, as they abandoned it in such a hurry, everything will have been left behind.' Trying to raise the spirits of his sodden companions, he added, 'Ladies, I think I can even smell tonight's dinner. Hot succulent roast chicken, baked potatoes with farm fresh beans.' Then licking his lips, added, 'Maybe even a glass of wine or two. A Châteaux like this always has a grand wine cellar. At its very worst, it's a dry roof for the night.'

'Or,' interjected Amelia, 'we will be arrested.'

'As always, Amelia, you are wise and it's right to be cautious. However, if we stay out here, pneumonia may have us and, if baby Jacinta is to have a chance, this is a time to be bold and brave. As that wonderful poem by Lord Tennyson says, "Into the valley of Death."' Breaking his cover from the trees, Artōrius strode forward. After a few steps he stopped, looked back at Emma and Amelia, who were still rooted to the spot and called in a powerful commanding voice, 'Forward, my Light Brigade,' before striding on. Amelia and Emma caught up with Artōrius in moments and, side by side, they approached the front door, which was ajar.

Once inside, Emma called out in a loud voice, 'Hello!' Her greeting echoed back from the stony silence of the empty house.

Peering at Artōrius questioningly, Amelia said, 'How did you know?'

'I cheated,' came the chuckling reply. 'I saw the door was open, and the flag wasn't hung properly.' He flicked the light switch, which was near where they'd entered, and the lights came on. 'We have power,' he said, subtly changing the topic.

Amelia was sure that Artōrius would not have been able to see the front door from where they were hiding in the trees, but her musings were diverted by the discovery of power, followed swiftly by thoughts of finding something dry to wear. As if reading her mind, Artōrius suggested, 'Let's check upstairs and see if we can't find something warm to change into.'

The first door they came to opened into a grand bedroom, with an elegant four-poster bed, the central piece. It had the appearance of a high-ranking officer's apartment rather than a room used as a brothel. The wardrobe bore out this truth. Inside hung a freshly pressed general's uniform beside an array of stylish and tasteful women's clothing. Along with formal wear, they found men's casual attire, but the ladies' wear was designed to impress and not suited for travelling or keeping its wearer warm.

Selecting a jacket and pants from the cupboard, Artōrius held them against himself. 'These will do nicely,' he declared.

Emma and Amelia would need to keep searching if they hoped to find more practical outfits.

'I'll meet you downstairs,' called Artōrius, as the women left the room. Neither answered, instead Emma raised her hand in acknowledgement as they departed down the hallway. Later, they found Artōrius in the kitchen, peeling potatoes. He glanced up as they entered. 'A little warmer?' he said brightly.

Emma and Amelia each wore dark blue woolly jumpers, black slacks, and comfortable shoes, while baby Jacinta was wrapped in a warm blanket. Artōrius thought they resembled sisters.

'Why don't you leave Jacinta with me while you set a nice warm fire in the sitting room? It's on the other side of the hall and looks cosy. I saw a wood pile as we came in and spotted raincoats next to the front door.' He dropped another potato into the pot of water with a plop. 'There's a basket over there,' he said, pointing towards the wall. 'Just Jacinta's size.'

Emma hesitated, she was unsure whether she wanted to leave her baby, not from fear — on the contrary, she trusted Artōrius, he was mysteriously reassuring — but a mother's guilt haunted her.

Sensing her unease, Artōrius said kindly, 'We all need to stay warm tonight. You're surely not expecting an old man like me to be lugging that wood about? Besides, I'm your master chef for this evening and, despite my prophecy, there's no chicken. You will have quail instead. Don't worry, Emma, I'll take good care of Jacinta.'

After settling the baby in the basket, Emma and Amelia went about their task of gathering wood and setting the fire.

Once they left the kitchen, Artōrius went to Jacinta and, closing his eyes, rested a hand on the child's chest. They had all become cold and wet during the storm and he secretly held grave fears for the baby's survival. *Good, good. You're a strong one*, he muttered aloud. *Yet I sense we must stay here awhile if you're to have a fighting chance. My young one, Amelia's child, is due soon. We must be gone before then, but for you, we will stay as long as we can.* With his eyes still closed and his hand feeling the gentle rhythm of her breathing, the baby's heartbeat synchronised with his and resonated throughout his body.

It took a while before the fire raged, but neither Emma nor Amelia noticed the passage of time. Once he heard the crackling of flames, Artōrius carried the baby into the sitting room, along with some pureed apple he had prepared for her. 'Stay and rest,' he said to them. 'For tonight, you dine as queens and I will be your servant.' Before returning to the kitchen, he gave a royal bow and added, 'My ladies, dinner will be served in half an hour.'

After feeding Jacinta and settling her down to sleep, Emma and Amelia relaxed into the comfortable chairs facing the roaring fire. The sound of the beating rain broke against the windows and the howling wind rattled the house as it strode noisily over the roof. They sat together in comfortable silence, listening to the wilds of the world outside as it went about its business. For the first time in many weeks, they both felt warm and safe. 'Would it be prying if I asked where you're from?' asked Amelia.

'Poland, Warsaw. It was such a beautiful city before the war. Now, it's like so many of the places we've seen, a site of death, rubble and destruction, like Dresden. Was that your home?'

'Yes, that's where I grew up. All of my family was there, but now everybody I loved is gone. Dead. After the bombing, I had to flee. To run. To run away. I suppose I am a coward for leaving.'

'No, Amelia, you're not a coward for wanting to live. Neither of us are cowards for running; we had children to protect.' Emma paused because, despite what she had just said, she too believed that she was a coward. Feeling a welling from deep inside, Emma wanted to confess her sins, not in search of absolution, for there was none to be had, but to unburden herself with the truth, though she had sworn to herself to keep the story secret. The past weighed heavy on her conscience, a tormenting millstone that would forever hang around her neck.

Emma sighed, then, with a voice that quivered in pain, said, 'I left Karl, my husband, in the hands of the Gestapo when I fled Warsaw. We were members of the Polish resistance, he a commander during the Warsaw uprising against the Germans. The Gestapo captured him, and he was being tortured to force him to hand over the names of others in the underground movement. He wouldn't turn. I visited him where he was being interrogated and saw how he was being miserably treated...so badly beaten. It was heartbreaking.'

Emma took a breath, trying to regain her composure before continuing. 'They allowed a visit because the Gestapo wanted me to tell our fellow resistance fighters what was happening, to frighten them, but Karl had vowed to me, no matter what they did to him, he would never betray his friends. Not long after that visit, the Gestapo rounded up all of our family, everyone. I was arrested along with Jacinta, who was only a couple of weeks old then. Jacinta and I were kept together in a separate cell, not in with the rest of our relatives.'

Emma took another gasp of air, and looking away from Amelia, spoke towards the fire. 'The next morning, I was taken to a courtyard inside the prison. Karl was already there, gagged, sitting with his hands tied behind a chair. In front of him was a table with a pen and paper on it. They made me stand beside him, alongside an SS officer, while the Gestapo watched.'

'In front, about twenty metres away, were our families, hands and legs tied, stood in a line, like the condemned facing a firing squad.'

"Good morning, Mrs Kowalska, the SS officer had pronounced." Emma paused. 'I can still remember his tone. It was a voice of a Sunday church picnic, not an execution. Like the older SS man who took you, Amelia. He said to me,'

"Your husband has proved himself stubborn, which I regret to say, for his family, is most unfortunate. I want you to understand what happens if people don't cooperate with us."

'He turned towards Karl and said in a grotesquely sweet way, "Mr Kowalski, I will ask you one more time to write down the names and addresses of your resistance associates."

'But you see, even if he wanted to, he couldn't, because Karl's hands were tied and a gag was in his mouth. The Gestapo officer came over and continued with the game, lifting the pen from the table and holding it towards Karl, before saying, "No? That's such a shame."

Emma swallowed. 'The Gestapo man nodded to the SS officer, who took a revolver from his holster, walked towards our family and shot Karl's parents, one after the other, and then his grandmother. My mother and father were next in line. Our other siblings had already been lost to the war. Other than Jacinta and me, Karl now had nobody left.'

"Mrs Kowalska, do you mind if I call you Emma?"

'The Gestapo officer had waited, as if he expected me to say something. When I didn't, he continued. "Emma, I think you know who your husband's associates are."

'He then nodded towards two of the soldiers who were also in the courtyard with us. They marched forward and, taking the arms of my parents, half led and half dragged them away. He grabbed my chin and inspected my face by moving my head from side to side. Looking into my eyes, he said with a haunting and deadly voice...' Emma stopped speaking to wipe the tears that were forming away. She continued.

'He said, "You're a pretty little thing. It would be such a shame if something were to happen to you. Emma, I want you to go home and write down the names of all the people you know who are participating in the uprising." I remember that he then looked at his watch and said, "At half-past three this afternoon, I will send my driver to collect you. If I am satisfied, you've been truthful, your parents will be free to go and, of course, you and the baby."

"Karl?" I asked. He replied.

"He will need to stay with us in prison. But he will live."

'Jacinta and I were driven home, but no one else in the resistance knew that we had been released.'

Emma paused again, looking towards Amelia before returning her stare to the fire and saying, 'I'm the real coward. What I should have done was to give

Jacinta to one of our friends and been taken back to the prison to be killed, along with my husband and parents. What I did instead was to run. The truth, Amelia, is that I was frightened of being tortured and witnessing Karl and my *matka* and *tata* being murdered.'

'I deserted, leaving them to certain death. Now, the Gestapo is after me. Jacinta and I only have each other and, because of what I did when the war is over, I can never go back. Never.'

Emma's story, apart from an occasional pause and swallow, was delivered mostly in a monotone and matter-of-fact way. The burden of a guilty woman.

Amelia sat motionless for a moment, not knowing what to say and worried; whatever words she chose would sound trivial and condescending. Should she say, 'It wasn't your fault,' or 'I would have done the same.' Perhaps she should just say, 'You were right to leave; they were going to kill you all anyway.' Instead, she settled on a question.

'How did you meet Karl?'

The query took Emma by surprise and made her smile as she was transported back in time to the beginning of their romance.

'He was ten years older than me, the older brother of one of my school friends, Natalia. It's difficult to pinpoint the exact time when things began to change between us. From an early age, he often escorted me home if I'd been to their place visiting Natalia. Then one day, I started hoping it would be him who would walk me home. On those times when I visited Natalia, and he was away at work, I felt quite dejected. I remember, it was when I turned sixteen, he asked my father if he could take me to the theatre. I'd been to the movies before with Karl, but always with Natalia as company. This was different. It was just him and me. He had a good government job and was so worldly. We would talk for hours and hours about all kinds of things and dream of the places in the world we were going to visit. It was on my eighteenth birthday that he asked my father for my hand in marriage. I can still remember waiting outside of the door, my heart racing, pacing up and down, petrified he would reject Karl's request. It wouldn't have mattered because I would have run off and married him anyway, but I loved my father and wanted his blessing. When the door finally opened, it was my father standing in the entrance and not Karl. His face was expressionless. He held his hand out towards me and beckoned me to take it before leading me inside. I looked to Karl, whose expression, like Father's, gave nothing away. I feared the worst and still remember how my heart began to sink.'

'He took me to the chair next to where he'd been sitting and said. "Sit, my dear," before asking Karl to leave. He then said.'

"Do you know Karl has asked for your hand in marriage?"

"Yes, Father," I answered.

"Is this what you want?"

"Oh yes, Father, more than anything else in the entire world."

"I see..." I still remember he paused, stopped speaking, and I was so worried, not knowing what he was going to say next. It was a question.

"Emma, my love, do you understand you won't always feel so giddy in love as you do now?"

'I said, "I will always love him as I do now, for ever and ever. However, I understand, Father, that love changes with time and that we must change with it. I see how much you love Mother, but I can also see it's different from how I feel about Karl. Nonetheless, it's still love. I want to be like you and Mother, and with Karl it will be."'

Emma smiled at Amelia as the warmth of the memory filled her. She continued.

'He took my hand again and, holding it in his, said to me, "If you are certain, my love."

"I am, Father, truly I am," 'I said, to which he replied, "Then, who am I to stand in the way. I consent with all my blessings for a happy and long life together.""'

'I can still remember the feeling when he said yes. Then he smiled and stared into my eyes, telling me not to forget my old father and making me promise to visit after I was married.'

'That was in 1940. With Germany having already invaded Poland, everything seemed more urgent, so we married three months later. Karl was still employed by the government, but now it was German, which is how he avoided conscription. But, at the same time, he was part of the underground resistance. They held meetings at our flat, fugitives stayed with us, so over time, we became more and more involved in the movement.'

'We agreed not to have children until after the war, but nature has a way of making up its own mind. Karl was the most wonderful and kind man and, it's my solemn promise, there will never be anyone else but him. When this wretched war is over, I'm moving to England to give Jacinta a new life, away from the past.

I never want her to know what happened to her father and our family. Or what I did. That is my secret, my sin which will haunt me until St Peter makes his judgement at the gates.'

'Through the resistance movement, I have a contact in England, you see.' Emma delved into her pocket and removed a tattered box of matches. Opening it so Amelia could look inside, there was a folded bit of paper. 'I've never met him, but when the war is over, I know he will arrange transport for me to England.'

'What will you tell Jacinta about her father?' Amelia asked.

'That he was a soldier fighting with the Germans and died, along with millions of others. About our family, I will tell part of the truth. They are all dead, casualties of war, but mainly I will say nothing because of my shame. Jacinta's life should not be burdened by my past, and I want her to marry and have many children. She will bring a new story for our family, the only history once my life is over.'

There was a sound at the sitting-room door, and Emma and Amelia turned to see Artōrius carrying a tray of steaming food. He placed it on a small table in the corner of the room along with a bottle of wine, announcing, 'Ladies, your dinner is served.'

None of them could remember when they had eaten such a feast; with war and rationing, such food wasn't available to ordinary folk. Since fleeing, most days had been spent fighting off starvation. Each enjoyed the banquet in quiet solitude and, when they had finished eating, having scraped the plates almost crystal clean, Artōrius suggested they adjourn to the chairs by the fire. 'Another glass of wine,' he proffered, topping up their glasses from dinner. He then joined them, removing from his pocket an old smoking pipe and, grasping the bowl, brought the pipe to his lips, whereby he gave three quick draws on its end, making popping noises with his lips as he did so. He had no tobacco and nor would he smoke in a room with other people present, but the pipe was a trusted companion of many a journey.

The conversation around the fire was easy but, unlike before, didn't stray into the personal, nor did it ponder the days to come. Emma was the first to suggest that she was going to retire for the night, having chosen a suitable room earlier. 'I won't be long behind you,' called Amelia as Emma left the room with Jacinta in her arms.

Looking at Amelia, Artōrius said, 'You should both get a good night's sleep. I'm going to bake some fresh bread for the morning, a treat for...' Before he could finish the sentence, he was distracted by a frightened Emma rushing back into the room.

Amelia, seeing Emma distressed, asked in a concerned voice, 'What's wrong?'

'I just saw a ghost on the upstairs landing.' Emma was expecting a question from Amelia, but it didn't come, so she filled the void: 'It was a little girl. One split second she was there, and the next gone. I definitely saw her.'

'How marvellous,' said Artōrius, with enthusiasm. His statement had the desired effect, immediately pacifying the ripple of panic that had crept into the room. 'Who would have thought,' he continued, 'that this house should hold such wonderful surprises? How old do you think she was?'

Emma thought for a moment. 'I'm not sure, about seven or eight. She was gone so quickly.'

'What was she wearing?' asked Amelia.

'A blue dress; it was so pretty. Her blond hair was hanging down on her back, almost as if someone had forgotten to tie it up.'

'Did you see where she went?' asked Artōrius in a reassuring voice, convincing Emma that he believed her story.

'Down the corridor. When I got there, the area was empty, all the doors were still shut. She had vanished into thin air.' Her gaze moved from Artōrius to Amelia. 'Would you mind if I shared your room tonight?'

Amelia stood up. 'Not at all. I was just going to bed myself. Will you be OK on your own?' she asked Artōrius.

'Who, me?' He chuckled. 'I was going to spend my night right here, by the fire and keeping it alight for the morning. If our new friend wants to join me, she would be most welcome.'

'You're not afraid?' asked Emma.

'Emma, my dearest one, if the ghost had intended to harm you, it wouldn't have run away. I think you gave each other quite a fright. Look at me. These old bones and weathered face are truly hideous. I reckon the young girl won't be disturbing me, nor anybody else tonight.'

'Sweet dreams and I will see you both in the morning for freshly baked bread – with butter. Can you imagine that?'

When they had gone, Artōrius returned to the kitchen and prepared the morning treat. The smell of freshly baking bread spread its inviting aroma throughout the house. When it was done, he removed it from the oven and carried it to the sitting room. Leaving the door ajar, he moved a small side table in front of the open fire and placed the bread on top. With the house cloaked in darkness, save for the flickering light of the flames, he sat in a chair in the corner of the room, mostly concealed by the shadows of the night. *Come, my little blue mouse*, he whispered to himself, as he waited patiently with his pipe as company.

It was two hours later, with the rest of the house having passed into slumber, when he heard the faint creaking sound of the sitting-room door being pushed further open. All fell silent again, and Artōrius imagined his small mouse scanning the room before venturing forth. He remained motionless. Moments later, there was the pitter-patter of little feet. A child, a small girl, came into view. Nervously, she reached for the bread.

'I baked that especially for you,' Artōrius said quietly.

Like a deer startled by the growling of a lion, the girl rose swiftly to her full height and swung her head toward the voice, ready to run.

'Don't be alarmed, my little one. I am a friend who's come to help you.'

'Did Mrs Rigby send you?' came a timid reply.

Artōrius knew what he said next was really important if he wanted to gain the child's trust. Lying was never his preferred option but, sometimes, if a lie could remove hurt, it was preferable to the truth. This was maybe one of those occasions. If he said the wrong thing and the girl suspected he was lying, she would run away and if, as he thought, she had been hiding in this house for a long time, she would prove difficult to find. In a split second he had to surmise how she came to be here and what was Mrs Rigby's role. 'Mrs Rigby had to leave suddenly and couldn't take you with her,' he said. 'She wanted to, but when she couldn't, she asked us, the ladies upstairs as well, to come and find you. It all happened so quickly that Mrs Rigby didn't even have a chance to tell us your name, only that we would find you here. She said you were a very brave girl, and you were to come with us on a grand adventure to find her.'

'Don't you know where she's gone?' came an inquisitive reply. Artōrius felt the child was gauging if he could be trusted.

'No, but that's what makes it a grand adventure. Mrs Rigby said you liked adventures. Is that true?'

'Oh yes, very much. It was the game Mrs Rigby and I played all the time. I had to hide and never be seen by anybody in the house. Mrs Rigby said, if I was, they would take me away, like my parents.' She sniffled as she uttered the words, and Artōrius guessed she was crying; in the firelight, he couldn't see her properly.

'What's your name, child?' he asked with an authority that made her feel safe and not scared.

'Hannah. Hannah Katz.'

'Hannah Katz.' The old man stood. 'My name is Artōrius. I am a great and noble knight who's been sent to rescue you.' Lifting his pipe above his head, Hannah envisioned, from one of her storybooks, a gleaming sword and a man clad in polished armour. The silhouette of a red lion adorned his chest, and his silver suit sparkled in the flickering firelight. 'Fear no more, Hannah, for I have come,' he declared.

Hannah ran to Artōrius, and as he wrapped his arms around her, she felt the strength of his embrace. In that moment, she sensed his power enveloping her, and felt safe.

'You must be hungry, my mighty mouse. Let me get you something, then it's time to rest. In the morning, you can tell me and my friends about your adventure.' He let go his embrace.

When Hannah stepped back, she saw Artōrius as an old man, but she wasn't afraid, because she knew his secret.

Artōrius went to the kitchen, fetching a plate, some water and jam, returned and, still with only the glow from the fire as light, sliced the bread and covered it liberally with a coating of sweet blackberry jam. After pouring a glass of water, he returned to his seat and watched her eat. When she had finished, he wiped Hannah's hands and face and said, 'It's time for rest, my mouse,' and led her to one of the chairs facing the fire. He then went back to his seat and retrieved a blanket he'd brought downstairs for himself, and tucked Hannah snugly in for the night.

As he stepped away, she asked, 'You won't leave me?'

'No, my princess. Old Artōrius will be in his chair, where he can keep a watching eye over all the kingdom. Sleep tight.'

CHAPTER 11

Peter Kramer

After the trip to Dresden, I busied myself with cleaning out the rest of Mother's house, in readiness for the sale, and working on what was to be my final journalist assignment.

It's astonishing how quickly the letters and Mother's half silver 5 Reichsmark coin drifted from my consciousness. It turned out the story wasn't finished with me.

Having spent the day in London following up on leads for my newspaper article, by the time I caught the train home, it was already eight thirty at night. I was hungry, having not found the time to eat before catching the train. Arriving home, I remember wondering if I should turn the computer on or make dinner. The desire to check my emails beat the hunger pains. There were a few messages waiting that needed attention, the obligatory spam, from sites I booked or bought things through, accompanied by a mix of unsolicited advertising. Glancing at the subject lines of each email, in a split second, I determined its fate. Delete or open. Most of my actions were delete, delete, delete. I reached one from "Forces War Records". I thought it would likely be an invitation to subscribe to whatever newsletters or databases they supported. I hesitated, not out of interest for their services, but because it reminded me of my query on the Wehrmacht Militaria Forum site, seeking information about Peter Kramer. Delete. The Forces War Records email went into the recycle bin. After a few moments of consideration, with some reluctance, I entered the Wehrmacht Militaria Forum into the search engine. That there was a message waiting for me was unsurprising; it was its contents that captured my imagination.

Dear Jacinta,

I served alongside Peter Kramer during the war, and he often talked about Amelia. As you may already know, she was tragically killed during the bombing of Dresden. How do I know this, you might ask? Peter told me.

From what we could piece together at the time, the Wehrmacht made a grave mistake. After a battle, Peter was injured but was also recommended for an Iron Cross for his bravery against the enemy. Somehow, an administrative mix-up occurred, and he was mistakenly listed as deceased. All his possessions were collected from the camp and sent to his family, along with the notification of his death.

The error was discovered after he was released from hospital and returned to our unit. Surprisingly, because of the mix-up, he was granted leave and travelled to

Dresden, arriving just after the February 1945 bombing. When Peter returned, he told me that Amelia, her mother and his family had all been lost in the raid.

I owe my life to Peter; he saved me and four other members of our unit from certain death, which is why he was recommended for the commendation. It was while helping us he sustained the injuries that hospitalised him.

Peter and I both survived the war and kept in touch intermittently for many years, though that now feels like a lifetime ago. The last I heard, he was a doctor in a town called Aberdeen, North Carolina. I imagine he has since retired and may have even moved away.

As you age, the memories from the past seem to grow in significance, not that I want to recall the brutal aspects of war. But the friends you had during those difficult times resonate stronger. I think because they were your brothers in arms and in death.

When I read your inquiry, it brought back the memories of when Peter would read Amelia's letters to me. Not always all she wrote. Sometimes he'd smile and say, 'This bit is just for me.'

It was the correspondence with Amelia that sustained Peter during what were trying times. The loss of her letters distressed him more than the Wehrmacht mistakenly pronouncing him dead.

It is because I know how dear those letters were to him that I write to you now. Although I no longer have his address, I'm confident he would want me to tell you all I know.

If he were still alive and you returned the letters to him, it would be nothing short of a miracle. I pray that this is your intention.

Yours truly,

Marcus Lawrence.

CHAPTER 12

Hannah

Hannah was helping Artōrius prepare breakfast in the kitchen when Emma and Amelia came in. 'Well, I never,' declared Emma, 'if it's not the young lady from the stairs.' Unease crept across Hannah's face, so Emma added, 'Would you like to see my baby? Her name is Jacinta.' Emma lowered the basket she was carrying so that Hannah could look inside. The distraction had the desired effect; Hannah became less anxious, but winning her trust took Amelia and Emma a couple more days. During that time, they learned she was six years old and had come to stay with Mrs Rigby when she was four. For reasons Hannah didn't fully understand, Hannah's mother brought her to the mansion because it was no longer safe in Berlin. Mrs Rigby had told her she had to be a brave girl and that one day her parents would return. The truth, at first, was too terrible to share: the Germans had taken her parents away.

Artōrius and Emma guessed that Hannah's family were Jewish, and that she was brought here to save her from the concentration camps. Amelia knew Jews had been rounded up and taken away but was indignant when told of the extermination camps with their gas chambers. For a moment, Emma seemed willing to let Amelia's ignorance pass, but so raw were her memories that she could not. Images of the Jewish ghettos of Warsaw, horrifying stories of the brutality and mass killings of those hideous camps that filtered back to the resistance, flooded her thoughts. She snapped in anger. 'You are telling me you did not know?'

Amelia opened her mouth, intent on defending herself and her country. She hesitated, staring at Artōrius, who said, 'It's true. I've seen it for myself. Not only Jews but anyone deemed undesirable by the Nazis: Gypsies, homosexuals, Jehovah's Witnesses, yes, even mentally and physically disabled Germans.

All were sent to be eradicated, the undesirable, the unwanted, any person seen as a burden on an Aryan race. The death toll will be into the millions.'

'I did know some of it, though I closed my mind to the stories, like many of us,' confessed Amelia, lowering her head, searching her soul for the truth. 'Early in the war, I remember reading in the papers that Hitler rid the Reich of the Jews. I did not know his plans extended to the other people, nor of the gas chambers for mass extermination. I'm ashamed to admit that there were rumours, but it was dangerous to question the false truth propagated, so I pushed it from my consciousness. I thought only of my life and how our family could survive, not the plight of those I didn't know. I've hidden behind ignorance, one of my own choosing, I know. I am truly sorry.'

Emma looked at Amelia. She was fuming as she said, 'How could anyone do that, choose not to know?'

'It's something we are all guilty of at some time, even you, Emma,' Artōrius said, his voice low and considered. He waited for a moment, in case Emma wanted to reply, but she seemed willing to let the old man talk. 'After our caravan was attacked by those warplanes, you encouraged Amelia to take a dead couple's pram. When she was drawn to their identity papers, you told her it was best not to know who they were. Stay disconnected, you meant. Choose not to know and hide the truth from your conscience. The circumstances are different, the process the same. We are all susceptible, all of us. That should be the lesson to the world from Nazi Germany. Information is manipulated, truth hidden, sheltering us from asking the troublesome questions. Only the very brave do that.'

***

It seemed not long after Hannah's fifth birthday, German soldiers had moved into the house. It was then Mrs Rigby told Hannah that, if she was seen, the soldiers would take her away, as they had done to her parents. At the end of the corridor upstairs, near where Emma first saw Hannah, was a secret passage leading to a hidden room. Inside was a bed, a small table with two chairs, reading material and colouring in books. A light bulb hung from the ceiling and there was a table lamp on the bedside chest of drawers. This, it seemed, was where Hannah had lived for the last year, with Mrs Rigby bringing food whenever she could. The room was as homely as solitary confinement could be, but they wondered how Hannah, in the long hours spent alone, had managed to keep her sanity and presence a secret. Fear, they considered; it had to be terror that kept a child of six quiet.

It was impossible to gauge from Hannah how long she had been alone. In her room there was no day or night, merely a light switch and visits by Mrs Rigby. Hannah told them she was usually ravenous by the time Mrs Rigby arrived. She had promised, however, no matter how hungry, she would never reveal herself. Then Mrs Rigby stopped coming. When Hannah heard people in the house, she thought they were soldiers and knew to stay hidden. Having not eaten for a long time, she was driven by hunger to come out of hiding. Artōrius reckoned, from the state of the food in the kitchen, that she'd been on her own for four or five days.

'What are we going to do with her?' Artōrius asked, expecting he already knew their answer.

'Find Mrs Rigby or her parents, if they're still alive,' Amelia asserted.

Emma agreed and then said, 'How, though? I mean, where do we start, when we know nothing about Hannah or Mrs Rigby?'

'Mrs Rigby's bedroom,' Amelia suggested. 'Hannah will know which one is hers. There may be some personal papers, a photo of herself, perhaps. If we're lucky, she will have kept letters from Hannah's parents showing their address.'

Artōrius recommended that they also search Hannah's hideaway too. 'That's where I would have hidden the things that I didn't want the Germans to find,' he said.

With Hannah as their guide, the next couple of days were occupied by the hunt. They discovered the house was used as a German officers' holiday retreat. From the examination of receipt and account books they discovered, they assessed that young women from local villages were paid as "Party Guests" for the house's visitors. The ledger told of women, picked up by a driver, brought to the house, then returned to the village at the end of the evening. It appeared some girls were frequent visitors, while others came only once.

The building had been requisitioned from its owner, Anna Rigby, who was subsequently paid to oversee the retreat's housekeeping services. With its parties, people coming and going, Artōrius thought it a miracle that Mrs Rigby had kept Hannah's presence a secret. They found nothing to explain why Anna Rigby had left. Privately, they all harboured the same fear. Who knew what secrets Anna would have learned? The skeletons in the cupboard, unsavoury events not to be disclosed. When the soldiers left, she was no longer needed and there was only one way to guarantee a person's silence!

Besides a few photographs, they discovered no personal documents belonging to Anna Rigby. Their dream of finding Hannah's parents' address was also shattered. 'We may have to leave her with the Red Cross,' suggested Emma. 'When the war is over, there will be thousands of people looking for their kin. It may be the best place for her.' Guilt tinged Emma's emotions as she spoke, but it was a luxury she could not afford. She was determined to make it to England and would not wait around for Hannah after the war. It might take years to find Hannah's family, she thought, even if they were still alive. Privately, Emma was struggling with her conflicting emotions. She didn't want to desert anyone else, but hard choices had to be made.

Emma was relieved when Artōrius said, 'Our future is too uncertain. I know of a good and trusted friend who will take care of Hannah until she can be reunited with her family, or find a new home. He lives close to our route and we will visit him when we set off again for Berlin.'

It was nearing the end of March and, for some days, Artōrius had been considering that the time was nearing to leave, especially as Amelia's baby was soon due. The comfortable home, filled with abundant supplies, had become a Shangri-La amidst a depraved war, merely delaying the inevitable decision to move on. The arrival of defeated and fleeing soldiers served as a catalyst, bringing a stark warning that the Red Army was advancing, intent on retribution. The men didn't stay or attempt to enter the house. They were on the run and, not long after their departure, the sounds of war could be heard in the distance. Their haven was about to transform into a dangerous place. Unbeknown to his companions, Artōrius had made preparations, placing provisions in a wheelbarrow ready for the trek ahead. Within half an hour of the appearance of the retreating battalions, the ragged troupe, swelled with the addition of Hannah, were once more heading towards Berlin, via Brandenburg, praying that they could keep west of the Russians. They abandoned their cross-country route to rejoin the road, and were shocked by the awaiting chaos. Confused people, soldiers and vehicles were moving in all directions; no one knew which way to run. A noose was tightening and there was no escape.

Artōrius's hands and arms ached from pushing the wheelbarrow, sometimes with only their meagre supplies on board but, more often than not, carrying one of their young companions, Hannah with her feet hanging over the front, or baby Jacinta lying on her back, staring up at the passing world. When he finally saw the township of Ziesar in the distance, Artōrius knew they had reached their target destination and they wouldn't make Brandenburg that day. 'We must find a place for the night,' he said. 'Brandenburg is twenty-five kilometres away. Tomorrow's walk.'

On the outskirts of town, they saw a derelict medieval building. 'Look,' Artōrius called to Hannah, who was walking while holding Amelia's hand. 'A castle, just the place for a noble knight and his princess.' She smiled.

The building was, as they'd hoped, deserted and, if it had been used for anything, it was long ago abandoned. The way in, through a stone archway, led to a central chamber and, if it hadn't been for a second storey fifty feet above them, it could have easily been mistaken as an abandoned cathedral. Something akin to a nave-like structure ran the length of the ground floor, from the entrance to the rear. Side-aisles, normal for a church, ran off either side of the nave. Unlike a religious building, the shape of a cross was absent. What was left of the daylight illuminated the inside, streaming through clear glass housed in ornate carved stone window frames. At the far end was a spiral staircase leading to the floor above and to whatever was below them as it curled downwards.

'I'm scared,' protested Hannah as they surveyed the inside of the building. Amelia gave her hand a reassuring squeeze. 'It's a beautiful castle,' she said, continuing with Artōrius's game.

'Hannah, why don't you and I go into town? There is someone I would like you to meet, then we can find our supper. A weary, helpless old man accompanied by his granddaughter, or so everyone would think. I wager that this will bring out the compassion and kindness of the townsfolk. While we're gone, you two should find a suitable place for the night, perhaps a smaller room that's not so draughty would be best. There's a torch and some candles in the barrow, but tread carefully if you explore upstairs, the floor could be rotten.'

Amelia remembered the conversation of days earlier, where Artōrius mentioned knowing a friend who could take care of Hannah. She wanted to ask if this was the person he was visiting and whether Hannah would return. She wanted to say goodbye. Amelia opened her mouth to speak, but Artōrius, seeing her, shook his head, and Amelia held her tongue.

As if reading her mind, Artōrius said, 'We won't be long. If my friend is home, we can all visit him tomorrow. Come, Hannah.' He stretched his hand towards the girl's and she took hold of it.

As they were leaving, Hannah asked, 'Who are we going to see?'

'You'll see.'

'A knight like you?'

'Better than a knight. He's a bishop.'

'A real bishop?' she asked excitedly.

'I've always called him "the Bishop" and bishops did once live in the church's residence, but, no, he's not a real bishop. He is a nobleman and a good friend whom I haven't seen in many, many years.'

The walk to an ancient red-brick, Gothic-style building took five minutes. The "Castel", as it was known, was exactly as Artōrius remembered. He wondered if the magnificent murals covering the chapel walls and ceilings had survived. He was here when the chapel had been consecrated and remembered richly painted depictions of iconic religious images. It had long since ceased being a place of holy worship but, as they passed through the arch and into the courtyard, the sense that this was still hallowed ground prevailed.

Letting go of Hannah's hand, he banged three times on the black wooden door. He expected the sound from his beating fist to be absorbed by the heavy timber; instead, his blows rang out, a command to those inside to come forth.

Artōrius and Hannah heard the door unlock before it creaked open, hesitantly partway. An elderly woman's face appeared in the gap, her features lined and creased, time etched into her skin. Frightened, Hannah clutched Artōrius's hand tightly, fearing she was looking at a witch.

'Yes?' the decrepit woman said, making it clear that visitors were not welcome here.

'Ms Charlotte Zimmermann, I see in my absence nothing has changed, you're as delightfully welcoming as ever. Is the Bishop in residence?'

'Bishop indeed, what nonsense is this?' Ms Zimmermann was about to say when recognition blossomed. 'Artōrius? Can it be, after all these years? Monseigneur,' she called out. 'Come quickly, it's Artōrius.' The door was opened wider and Charlotte brushed Hannah aside in her rush to embrace Artōrius. After her greeting, she stared at Hannah and said, 'Who might this fine young lady be?'

'I'm Hannah,' came a timid reply.

'What a beautiful name you have. Welcome, Hannah, a friend of Artōrius is always welcome here. Please come in.'

From inside the entrance hall, the Monseigneur was nowhere to be seen. Pointing to a room down a corridor on the right, Charlotte said, 'He will be in his study. He wouldn't have heard me calling, a little deaf nowadays, sometimes selective, but not always.' As they approached the doorway, they paused, and Charlotte said, 'Go on inside. I can't wait to see the expression on his face.'

It was forty-six years ago when Artōrius last saw his friend. He wasn't a Monseigneur then, but Charlotte was still his housekeeper. He had aged considerably, Artōrius thought, as he studied him from the doorway. Yet for a man of seventy-five years, aging was treating him kindly. 'Bishop John,' Artōrius called out.

The Monseigneur looked up from his work. For a moment, there was no sign of recognition on his face. Squinting his eyes, as if scrutinising the fine details of a rare piece of art, he said, 'Artōrius?... Father be praised, I can't believe it. You haven't aged a day in all these years.'

'Neither have you, John,' lied Artōrius.

'Nonsense, we both know that is not true. It's good to see you after all this time. What brings you to my humble abode? Charlotte, tea, if you will, and some of that cake we have been keeping for special occasions.'

'Yes, Monseigneur.'

Monseigneur John pulled himself up from his desk and embraced Artōrius. Next, he was introduced to Hannah and formally shook her hand. 'Sit,' he said, pointing towards the centre of the room and an old leather sofa with an accompanying armchair.

Having taken tea and reflected upon the years that had passed, Artōrius came to the matter at hand. He explained to Monseigneur John how he'd met Emma, Jacinta and Amelia on the road from Dresden and of the house where they discovered Hannah. The Monseigneur said that he knew of the German officers' retreat, because young girls from the village had often been invited there.

'We have endured difficult times, John, and many of the horrors of this war have yet to be fully revealed,' Artōrius said. 'As Germany collapses, we will be further dismayed by what lies ahead—raw depravity, mark my words. Hannah must be reunited with her parents, but the road to Berlin I must travel will not be safe for someone so vulnerable. Of all the people in the world, it is you, Monseigneur, that I trust to keep her safe until order is restored. When the war ends, I know you will work tirelessly to find her family.'

The Monseigneur nodded.

Artōrius said. 'I've heard from the lips of the wind, my friend, that the Castel is a place of sanctuary and hope for many children, with you as their guardian. The time for hiding is almost over, but not yet. I ask if there's room in the inn for one more?'

Smiling, the Monseigneur rose, asked them to follow, and led them down to an ancient catacomb that ran below the chapel and residence. He pushed against what seemed to be a solid brick wall and a secret door opened. Inside, the subterranean gallery, recessed for tombs, had been converted into primitive but homely living quarters. From the entrance, Hannah could see a row of beds. An older child, perhaps eleven, she thought, was reading to eight children who listened attentively. The older girl stopped when she saw the Monseigneur. 'Father,' she said, standing.

'It's OK, Jenny. A false alarm. Our visitors were friends. Excellent job, children. You were all hidden within two minutes. He gestured with his hand to his companions. If she wishes, we will add a new member to our gang. This is Hannah.' Hannah gave a shy wave. 'It's safe to come out now,' he said to the children, 'but stay alert for the bell.'

Speaking softly to Artōrius, the Monseigneur said, 'They are all children of parents taken to the camps. There were so many. I wish I could have done more.'

'You know that I'm a religious man, John, and so believe the Bible when it writes, *He who saves a single soul saves the world.*' Artōrius abruptly stopped talking and his eyes became alert.

'What's wrong?' asked the Monseigneur, aware of his friend's unease.

'I don't know, but I sense Emma and Amelia are in difficulty and need me. We must leave you now.

Hannah and I will return tomorrow and, if she wishes,
Hannah will join you.'

CHAPTER 13

America

I read the forum message a couple more times and was surprised by how angry I felt. Peter Kramer had survived the war; how on earth could they make such a huge mistake and not correct it? Yet, when I considered the millions that had been killed, and the complete breakdown of society, it was probably an understandable error. Having decided to push Peter and Amelia from my consciousness, they were back and it was the words of Marcus Lawrence that weighed heavily.

> If he were still alive and you returned the letters to him, it would be nothing short of a miracle. I pray that this is your intention.
>
> Yours truly,
> Marcus Lawrence.

After mulling over and rereading the message several times, I picked up the phone and called international directory assistance, not expecting much. 'Can I have the number for Peter Kramer in Aberdeen, North Carolina, America?' To my surprise, within seconds, I was jotting down the contact details on a piece of paper. Now what? It was nearing ten o'clock at night, I muttered to myself. Too late to call now. Having travelled to the USA for work on several occasions, I knew it wasn't late at all; in fact, it was the perfect time—four in the afternoon.

'Hello, my name is Jacinta Kowalska, I'm calling from the United Kingdom – England. I'm looking for a Peter Kramer, a friend of Marcus Lawrence, they served together in the Second World War. I'm terribly sorry if I've rung the wrong person, but the last we knew of Peter, he was living in Aberdeen. North Carolina and you're the only P. Kramer in the phone book.'

After hesitating, he said, 'Yes, I am that Peter. Do I know you?'

My heart raced. I'd found him, the man in the letters. 'No, sir, we've never met, but I discovered a bundle of letters which I believe belong to you. They are between a Peter Kramer and Amelia Huber of Dresden from the Second World War. I also have letters written by Amelia to Peter Kramer, and a telegram to Peter's family from the Wehrmacht, saying that he was killed.' The phone went silent. It was a slow ten seconds before he spoke again.

'I'm sorry, I'm stunned. It was all such a long time ago, and Amelia was killed when Dresden was bombed.'

'Yes, sir, I discovered that, when I visited Dresden, to see if I could find her or a living relative.'

'May I ask... Jacinta, wasn't it?'

'Yes.'

'How do you come to be in possession of these letters?'

'It's a mystery and one I was hoping you may help me with. I found them in a shoebox, in a cupboard, when cleaning out my mother's house, in preparation for its sale. You see, she's recently moved into a care home.'

'What's your mother's name?'

'Emma Kowalska, her maiden name was Debska. She was from Poland. My father, Karl Kowalski, was killed fighting in the Wehrmacht. I think she was in Dresden during the bombing.'

'No, I'm sorry, I don't recall anybody by those names. Have you asked her?'

'She refuses to speak about the war, which I understand. It was traumatic for her, so there's little point asking her unless I already know the answer. Mother would say, "Oh those old things, I found them somewhere, but can't remember when." She would add. "I'm surprised I haven't thrown them out already."'

'Oh, I see. That would make it difficult.'

'Would you like me to post them to you?' But before he could answer, I said, 'One other thing, in the box there are some old photographs. I was wondering if I email them, you might recognise the people?'

'I'm afraid I don't have a computer, a bit of a dinosaur. You could post copies. Yes, if it were no trouble, I would like to have the letters. I don't know if you're interested, but there was never anybody else after Amelia. So, to have those letters would mean a lot. You would be doing me a great favour if you could send them.'

Even though I had offered to send the letters, his comment still caught me off-guard and my mouth uttered the words before they hit my consciousness, 'I could bring them to you in person. Perhaps, if I wouldn't be prying, you might share some of your story with me. I am very interested.' Fearing I was pushing the boundaries, I added quickly, 'Please say no, if you don't think it's appropriate.'

'Do you suspect there may be a connection between what you have found and your mother?'

'In all honesty, I don't know what to suspect. I'm a journalist. Perhaps that leaves one with an inquisitive mind.'

'To travel all of this way, you must be a generous woman. I do not see a connection, but if my story can help, I would be happy to share it with you. You must bear in mind it was all such a long time ago now and my recollections are not as they once were.'

Before leaving for the United States, I drove to the care home to see Mother, debating whether to mention the letters or that Peter Kramer was alive. Having only recently returned from Germany, Mother expressed her displeasure at my departure with complaints like, 'Who's going to take me to my appointments?' and 'You're never home.'

Ignoring her jibes, I plucked up the courage to ask about the shoebox. 'While I was packing up your home, I found a shoebox in the cupboard containing old letters and photographs.' I paused, hoping my words would elicit a response. She looked blankly back at me, seemingly unaware of my conversation. 'Your World War Two identity card was also in the box along with these letters between a Peter Kramer and an Amelia Huber. They are such lovely letters; I was wondering who these people were.' I was about to ask if she knew them but stopped myself, because a closed question would allow her the escape of replying a simple, "No."

'Jacinta, you know I don't like recalling those times. If you must know, I met Amelia in Dresden. She had lost her entire family. Before she died, she gave me the letters and pictures.'

'In Dresden?'

'Yes. That's all I'm going to say, so please don't ask me again. Do you have them with you?'

'No.'

'I would like them. It's a vow I made.'

Stupid, I thought, annoyed with myself. *Now what am I going to do?* I'd promised the letters to Peter. But there was something else bothering me. How could Mother know Amelia Huber, a person killed during the bombing of Dresden? Mother was in Dresden around the time of the bombing. I knew that, but was she there long enough to develop a relationship with Amelia to be given her most treasured possessions? I felt sure I was missing something. Was my mother lying? A lightbulb moment struck me. If Amelia and her family were both killed in the Dresden bombing raid, then she couldn't have, as Mother had just said, given her the letters and photos after losing her family. Amelia was presumably already dead! Unless, of course, the records were wrong and Amelia wasn't killed.

Now I knew for certain Mother was hiding something. I hoped the truth would be found with Peter Kramer in the United States.

'OK, when I'm back from America, I'll see if I can find where I put them.'

Leaving the care home, I felt emboldened and righteous in pursuit of the facts. Reflecting on it now, I wondered if my motivations weren't vindictive, wanting to punish Mother for failing to share her secret. While I understand that lying can be for a greater purpose, the compassion, welfare or safety of others, I could comprehend no reason for her lying to me.

I arrived in Aberdeen mid-afternoon the day before meeting Peter Kramer. My immediate impression was that this was one of those towns best described as a hidden gem, with notable historical architecture, longleaf pine forests and a beautiful park with a walking track surrounding a lake.

We agreed to meet the next morning at ten thirty at the Bake House on S Poplar Street. 'You can't miss it,' Peter had said. 'It's opposite the Sewer Department.' When I asked how I would recognise him, he laughed, saying, 'If being over bloody eighty doesn't give me away, just ask at the counter, I'm a regular.'

I arrived early and felt surprisingly nervous as I found a table while comforting the battered shoebox.

'Jacinta?' asked a male voice.

Looking up, I saw an older man standing next to my table, Peter Kramer, for sure. He looked distinguished, a tall man of over six feet, once quite athletic, clean shaven with well-groomed silver hair. For a man of his age, he had remarkably smooth skin, fewer wrinkles than expected of a person of over eighty years of age. Standing, I said, 'Peter?' He nodded, and we shook hands before I invited him to join me.

Peter Kramer was articulate and well-spoken, as one would expect from a doctor. He confirmed my suspicions. The photograph of the girl and boy were of himself and Amelia. The one of the boy, in army uniform, was also him. The third was of Amelia with her mother and father. He read each of the letters in turn, often smiling as he mouthed the words. Occasionally he stopped, looking at me and said, 'Perhaps a little too much information, but we were both young. Who would have thought that someone else would read them?' After finishing the last letter, he leaned back in the chair and recounted their childhood together in Dresden. As I expected, he was from a poor family. Amelia's father was a tailor, so they were better off, but not wealthy. Nevertheless, as the war dragged on, both families struggled to make ends meet. He spoke of Amelia's father, Hans Huber, being called up to fight, not long before he was himself. He remembered how Hans's death, on the Russian front, had devastated both his wife Maria Huber and daughter Amelia.

Peter picked up the photographs of Amelia and himself together and, as he stared at them, said, 'You wouldn't believe how nervous I was writing the first letter, asking Amelia to be my girl, as we Americans would say.' He put down the pictures and, taking the second letter, said, 'My relief was immeasurable when she said that she would. Even now, I feel Amelia's pain from this letter, telling me of her father's death. You see, Jacinta, I was as close to Hans as I was to my father, so his loss came as a great shock. I remember

227

this letter more than any other. Of being torn between the grief of Hans death and the overwhelming joy of the revelation from Amelia's love. After reading it, I had a driving desire to be home and, as you know, I was granted a week's leave. When I saw Amelia, we both knew that the rest of our lives would be spent together. As you see from the letters that followed, Amelia was pregnant, and we planned to marry when the war was over, but none of that was to be.' He sighed.

'When you spoke to me over the phone, you said that Marcus wrote of the administrative mix-up that resulted in my family being told that I was dead. My personal effects were sent back to them in Dresden. As I understand it, my name had been given to the commander to be recommended for a bravery medal but ended up in the letter pile for those killed in action. When my gear was collected to be returned to my family, my army friends assumed I had died in the hospital. When I was discharged back to my unit, the mistake was picked up. Even though the war was going badly at that stage, I was given a week's leave to see my family. I arrived in Dresden the day after the bombing to find that mine and Amelia's family homes had been destroyed. I learned from surviving neighbours that our parents had refused to leave their homes. The day before I was to return to my army unit, Amelia was identified among the rubble. I never saw her, but they found her body along with her identity papers. How anyone would come to have the letters, I don't know.'

'I went back to the war front numb. I wanted to die, to be with Amelia and the others I loved. When I didn't, I promised to dedicate my life to the betterment of others, to the saving, rather than the taking of life. My journey to America is a story for another day. Let's just say that it was by good fortune and the genuine kindness of a few special people that I came to be here. The first few years were tough. I earned barely enough to pay the rent and feed myself. You can imagine Germans weren't the most popular race at the time. I pretended to be Austrian and learned to read and write in English with vigour, practising pronunciation to lose my accent as much as I could. I went to university and became a doctor, moving to this wonderful town over forty-five years ago. Then, out of the blue, you call. Here we are, with letters that I thought long ago lost or destroyed.'

I listened intently to Peter's story, but realised that he was adding little to what I knew already. I wondered if he too was being economical with his story, perhaps cautious? Was he holding something back, waiting to see what else I had to say, before revealing all, or was that my fantasy?

'You said that your mother's identity documents were also in the box. Are they here?'

'Yes.'

'Would you mind if I looked at them?'

I handed Peter the card. He studied the photograph. 'She was a beautiful woman, your mother.' He looked disappointed before adding, 'As I have said before, I've not heard of her and neither do I recognise her. Did you ask how she came to possess the letters?'

'She said Amelia gave them to her.' If I was expecting him to be shocked that they knew each other, he didn't show it, but from his questions, I knew his curiosity was sparked.

'Did you tell your mother that you were coming to see me?'

'I thought about it and decided not to until I'd spoken to you.'

Peter smiled. 'I feel like I'm interrogating. Please tell me to stop if you're feeling uncomfortable. That's not my intention.'

'Please, ask away.'

'I was wondering, Jacinta, how was it you came to discover the shoebox your mother kept hidden for all these years?'

I remembered he had already asked me this question over the phone, but it wasn't polite to say so. 'After moving Mother into a care home, the house needs to be sold. Everything has to be cleared out. If it hadn't been for the half silver 5 Reichsmark coin, I might have tossed the shoebox out, without taking its lid off, but I–'

Peter interrupted. 'I don't think you've mentioned the coin before.'

'No. I'd almost forgotten about it. With the letters and discovering that you hadn't been killed, it had slipped my mind. Where to start?' I took a deep breath. 'She has always worn a chain around her neck. I noticed it when I was a child but, if I knew then what hung on the necklace, I had forgotten. It was the day Mother moved into the care home. She discovered the necklace was missing and became quite distressed. When I suggested I would look for it the next day, she virtually demanded that I went and search for it immediately. Mother said to me it was all that she had.'

'I went back to the house and searched high and low for it. It had fallen into a pair of shoes that were next to her bed. Uncovering that she had worn half of a German coin for all these years came as a surprise.

Though I had discovered a part of her secret, I knew Mother would be reluctant to share any details and I was not to be disappointed. She refused to explain further. The best I could glean from her was that it was a substitute for the wedding ring they could not afford, a token from my father, who wore the other half. Hard to believe. She has worn it throughout her life and wishes to be buried with it.' When I'd finished speaking, I scanned his face for clues, anything to suggest that he knew something of this silver German coin. There were none, only the look of a person listening, trying to understand.

'That's a wonderful story. They must have been very much in love, like the people in these letters. Can you tell me about your father? You said that he was killed in the war?'

'No, not really. His name was Karl Kowalski. I think he was from Warsaw, in Poland, which is where he met and married Mother. Somehow, he ended up in the Wehrmacht and was killed. Towards the end of the war, Mother, with me as a baby, fled the advancing Red

Army and travelled to Dresden. That's where she must have met Amelia. After that point, I know nothing more, except that their families were killed during the conflict. To the best of my knowledge, I have no living relatives. Can I be honest with you, Peter? She's hiding something.'

'Is that not her privilege? She has witnessed much more than your generation will ever see, hopefully.'

That knocked the wind out of my sails. Peter was correct. It was her right but, even so, I countered with, 'Don't you think I deserve to know about my father?'

'Why, of course, but you're assuming there is more to know.' He paused for a second before continuing: 'You must excuse me, Jacinta. I find, in my later years, that I tire easily. When are you returning to Britain?'

'On Wednesday, but I'm meeting a friend tomorrow in Charlotte, before flying home the next day. I came to the USA to give you these letters, that's all. If I can make a confession; when I told Mother I'd found the letters, before coming here, she asked for them back. They really belong to you, however.'

'Would you join me for dinner tonight before you leave? I think you know my address.'

'Thank you, that would be my pleasure.'

'In the meantime, Jacinta, why don't you hold on to those letters and photos, until this evening.' He stood, gave a slight bow and said, 'It's been truly a pleasure and you've warmed an old man's heart by coming all of this way. This evening, if you're interested, I could tell you about Amelia's family.'

'And yours?'

'If you would like, and maybe some stories of Amelia and me as children. In exchange, you must share your experience of growing up in England. We could trade tales of our lives.'

'I would very much like that.' The sense he'd been holding something back passed, and I put my initial feelings down to the normal processes of building trust. As he was leaving, I called after him, 'I'm sorry, Peter, but I've just remembered, I think there's another letter that I've misplaced.'

'That's OK, Jacinta. I never thought I would see any of these again.'

'I have wondered if there were other letters. I mean, is this all of them?'

He thought for a second before answering. 'Notes rather than letters. I regularly sent Amelia money and always scribbled a little something.'

***

Peter lived in a quintessential American country home, white picket fence, green roof with a lovely veranda, where he was seated waiting for me to arrive. 'Can I get you something to drink, a glass of wine or something soft?' he asked.

'That would be lovely, white wine if you have it.'

'Please, make yourself at home. I thought we could sit outside for a while before dinner.' He returned a couple of minutes later carrying two glasses of wine and placed them on the small round table in front of me, before sitting in the chair on the other side. 'You can see why I stayed. It's a wonderful little town - the people are friendly, and it's very pretty. I particularly love walking around the lake. Have you seen the lake?' I nodded. 'I was the only doctor when I came here; how many of the townsfolk I've brought into this world, I've lost count. As I have said this morning, like many people who survived the war, I felt I had an obligation to give back to society, particularly true having been a German soldier. We all have our secrets, Jacinta; one of mine is that I was from Germany and not Austria. Would the good folk of Aberdeen care where I was from now? No, but they would feel disappointed, maybe angry, that I have lied to them all this time. When I came here forty-five years ago, being German would have mattered. Sometimes skeletons from the past best remain there.'

Peter went on to share memories of growing up in Dresden, recounting the wonderful times he had with Amelia. How Amelia embroiled them in the black market, inadvertently Peter told me, blushing, stealing and selling objects for food or money. Both family homes had been destroyed, so the pictures I brought with me were the only ones in existence of Amelia, her parents and him before leaving to fight in the war. He recalled the solemn vow and promise Amelia and he had made when he asked her to marry him, that no matter what happened, neither of them would have another. 'It's a pledge I've kept with no regrets. I've had hundreds of children, brought them into the world, seen them grow up and then brought their children's children into the world. I've never been lonely and feel blessed to have lived. Enough of me. Tell me about your mother and you.'

By the end of the evening, I felt truly humbled to have met a remarkable man whose only desire appeared to be doing good for others. I also felt sorry for him, for having to disown his own heritage, keeping his own story untold. I had always toyed with the idea of writing a book and wondered if unravelling my mother's story could be a part of it. After meeting Peter, I realised that the truth was not always mine to tell. When I went to leave the letters and photos with Peter, he surprised me by saying, 'They belonged to your mother.' Adding, 'If I were to give you something and ask you not to open it, will you honour that promise?'

I looked at him, confused, before saying, 'Sure.'

'It's a gift for your mother, for so diligently honouring Amelia's wishes. I don't know if she will share it with you. That is something that has to be her decision.'

'You know the truth, don't you?'

'I suspect the truth, or at least part of it, but it's her story and her story alone. We must both respect that, just as I've asked you to respect my secret.'

CHAPTER 14

Loyalty

Amelia and Emma watched as Artōrius and Hannah departed before deciding to explore the building in search of the best place to spend the night. Emma had briefly considered leaving Jacinta to sleep where they were, but ultimately chose to keep her strapped to her back as they searched their The rooms on either side of the ground-floor nave offered no better protection. None had fireplaces, and all had broken windows, making them barren and cold even with their doors closed. Emma suggested they search upstairs.

The wooden staircase leading up into the distance looked sturdy as Amelia shone the torchlight left to right, then up and down. Cautiously, she climbed, testing each of the first sixteen steps by transferring all her weight to the front foot before moving to the next.

She paused at the first landing. The old wood had creaked and groaned under her weight, but she thought it solid. 'It's OK,' she called down. Emma joined her on the landing and together they ascended the rest of the way to the second storey. While downstairs resembled a church, with its open central space, upstairs was akin to the working area of a university or priory. A wide corridor with stone windows opened before them and they saw the remnants of bookcases or display cabinets on either side. Three doors, unevenly spaced, punctuated the right wall of the corridor.

'This was once a magnificent building,' Amelia observed. 'But look.' She let the beam of the torchlight fall on the wooden floor. Along the passageway, they spotted pieces of timber that were missing, exposing the level below.

'Too dangerous?' Emma asked.

'I think so. Yes, definitely.'

At the bottom of the wooden staircase, closer towards the outer wall, were spiral stairs, carved from stone, leading to the level below. The ascent had been fifty feet, but the descent seemed further, possibly an illusion caused by the confined space of a stone wall surrounding the narrow spiral staircase.

They were expecting the lower level to be in darkness, but it wasn't; how the faint light dimly lit the entire area was a mystery, a mastery of stone masonry long since forgotten. Before them appeared a magnificent crypt, its arches and vaults carved. The penetrating cold present upstairs was missing down in the depths. It was a sight to behold, and it momentarily took their breaths away. Drawn into the inviting crypt, they scanned in awe the ornate ceiling above as they walked onwards. In front of them, an area of stone floor was covered in timber. It wasn't hidden and, if Amelia had been watching where she placed her feet, she would have seen it easily.

The first she knew of its existence was when the ground below her collapsed. As the floor gave way, Amelia let out a scream and Emma turned to see her falling through the rotten timber covering an abandoned pit. At the last second, Amelia thrust out her hands, grabbing the edge, while her legs dangled into the abyss below.

Crying, she moved her legs in panic, hoping they would find purchase, but the wall was smooth. As she fidgeted, her fingers began to slip. With Jacinta strapped to her back, Emma threw herself to the ground, grabbing hold of Amelia's shoulders. With all of her strength she pulled, but Amelia didn't move.

'Help me,' Amelia called, as one of her hands dropped from the edge. Her body drifted downwards and Emma, still holding on, was pulled towards the pit. With nothing to secure her, if Amelia fell, Emma and Jacinta would also be dragged into the void and certain death.

Amelia's dangling hand found the edge again, and she hung on, but knew it wouldn't be for long. 'You have to let go,' she sobbed.

'I can't. I can't let it happen again.'

'You must think of Jacinta. She will fall with you, if you don't let go.'

Rather than let go, Emma edged forward and wrapped her arms under Amelia's shoulders. She pulled with all her might, but, with her main body mass now close to the hole, rather than lifting Amelia free, she felt herself being pulled further towards the pit.

'Let go,' Amelia screamed. 'I can't hold on any longer. Please, Emma, let me go. The war can't take all of us. Promise me, Emma, that you will live.' Amelia lifted her head to look into the eyes of her friend, but saw they were closed. She knew then they were all destined to die together, so tried to close her eyes as well. She failed, instead she stared into the solid wall of the pit. Breathing deeply, gathering herself together, Amelia searched for peace before unfolding her fingers.

Amelia was surprised by the sound of a voice which broke the expectant silence which accompanies the last moment. 'OK, Emma, wriggle back a bit. We can take an arm each.' Emma did as she was told. 'On the count of three, we pull. Ready.' It wasn't a question. 'One, two, three, pull. Again, pull.' As Amelia moved up a few inches, all her weight was held by her rescuers. 'Rest. Amelia, when we pull again, try to get your elbows over the edge, then you'll be able to help us. One, two, three.' Artōrius and Emma heaved again and Amelia planted her elbows against the rim of the pit, trying to lift herself as they pulled; she was stuck. 'Rest,' Artōrius commanded for the second time while holding on to Amelia securely.

'I'm wedged, something is holding me back,' said Amelia, anxious.

'Something,' retorted Artōrius, as if he didn't have a care in the world. 'You've got one hell of a belly and in it, a lifetime of responsibilities. We are going to give it one more try with all our strength this time. Are you ready?' No one answered. 'I said, are you ready?'

'Yes,' they all called in unison, including Hannah.

Amelia was free. Exhausted, they all lay motionless on the ground. 'You're a brave and strong girl, Hannah,' Artōrius said, breaking the silence. 'We couldn't have done it without you. Will you promise me you will look after my good friend, the Monseigneur, the same way?' She nodded her head. 'Good girl.'

Amelia, with tears streaming down her face, crawled to Emma and, putting her arms around her, said, 'You were going to die for me. I will never forget that. Never, I promise, Emma, never.'

After their ordeal, despite the chill in the air, they opted to sleep in one of the ground-floor rooms. As the women drifted into a deep slumber, Artōrius felt a stirring sense of urgency; Amelia's baby was on the verge of arrival. They would need to find a hospital, and their journey to Brandenburg had to begin at first light the next morning. There would be no time for long goodbyes, so he would take Hannah to the Monseigneur before the others awoke. They would leave for Brandenburg as soon as he returned. He knew that Emma and Amelia would be heartbroken at not being able to say goodbye to Hannah, but Amelia's baby had to take priority. Artōrius hoped they would understand.

CHAPTER 15

Brandenburg

They arrived in Brandenburg in late afternoon. The city had been bombed the night before and they were greeted by destroyed buildings and smouldering fires. If once there had been any semblance of order, chaos now ruled supreme, with as many people arriving as fleeing. Like on the road, no one, it seemed, knew which way to run. The only certainty was that the war would soon be over and the Red Army, not the British or Americans, would enter the fair city.

Amelia's labour pains started shortly after midday and Artōrius had abandoned what little possessions they still owned from the wheelbarrow and pushed her like a man possessed towards the city. Despite Amelia's protests, Emma insisted she take her identification documents so she wouldn't be turned away from the maternity hospital. Nearing the hospital, they came across a block of flats that had been partially bombed. Artōrius asked Emma to knock on the still intact ground-floor flats, to see if they were abandoned. Most, it seemed, had been.

'Number 5, do you see it?' He pointed the wheelbarrow containing Amelia towards the door where Emma, with Jacinta, were now standing. 'I'm going to take you to the hospital now, but this is where we will wait for you.' Amelia looked at Artōrius with concern. 'Don't worry, my precious one, I expect to collect you, but just in case, it's number 5.'

'Please, Artōrius, stay with me at the hospital until the baby is born. I'm scared.'

He looked at Emma, who nodded. 'We'll be safe here, Artōrius, stay with Amelia.'

'The Russians will be here any time and it won't be safe for you to be on your own, not for the first couple of days, not until things settle down. Promise me, Emma, that you will stay inside.'

'I will.'

'The hospital is around the corner. Once I've settled Amelia, I'll return with food.' He looked at her sternly. 'Promise me again, and lock the door.'

'Don't worry, Artōrius, I'll lock the door and wait.'

He nodded. 'OK then, let's go,' he said and pushed Amelia the rest of the way to the hospital.

If they feared being turned away, that evaporated the moment they arrived. Pushing her through the main entrance, they were greeted by a sour-faced matron wearing the Red Cross badge with a swastika inside. 'What on earth are you doing? Get her out of that wheelbarrow at once.' She helped Amelia stand.

'I think I'm having a baby,' Amelia cried, with her face red from exhaustion and the pain of the contractions.

'You think... child! I'm sure you're having a baby. Take short breaths and pant for me while we get you to the ward.' Leading Amelia by the hand, the matron began guiding her. Artōrius set down the barrow and began to follow, but she turned and, in the sternest tone she could muster, said, 'And where do you think you're going?'

The tone was such that it even rattled Artōrius. 'She wants me to stay with her.'

'Are you the father?' demanded the matron, looking him up and down as if in disgust.

'No.'

She pointed to a row of seats on the right, further down a corridor. 'You can wait there.'

Looking back at Amelia, her tone changed once again. 'What's your name, my child?'

Remembering the identification documents that she was carrying, she said, 'Emma.'

'Ah, Emma, I have a favourite aunt called Emma. She's really pretty, just like you are,' said the matron, trying to distract Amelia from her contractions.

Artōrius listened intently, watching as they vanished deeper into the hospital. He longed to sit, but found himself pacing anxiously like an expectant father. Outside, the sounds of war began to creep back into Brandenburg, a haunting reminder of the chaos unfolding beyond the walls. Occasionally, the hospital walls would shake.

Even here won't be safe, he thought.

As soon as Amelia's baby was born, he knew they should seek shelter at the flat, a place unlikely to attract attention. His promise to return that evening with supplies for Emma and Jacinta had been forgotten until the matron returned to dismiss him.

'Come back tomorrow. I'll take good care of her. Since it's her first, I suspect we're in for a long night.'

'Is Emma alright?' Artōrius asked.

'Yes, nothing to worry yourself about...' The wall shook with the sound of a nearby explosion. 'The first one always takes a little longer but, luckily for her, we still have some gas that will keep her comfortable. You look as if you've been on the road?'

'Yes, we've walked from Dresden, trying to keep one step in front of the Russians. We're heading for Berlin.'

'I see.' The face of the matron was still sour, but she spoke now with the kindness she had shown Amelia. 'Do you have a place to stay?'

'We do.'

'Is it nearby?'

'Very, just a couple of blocks away.'

'Very good. What about provisions for the baby?'

'No, and this will be the second baby in our little troop. I'm travelling with another young mother.'

'I see... Wait here.'

With the precision of a drilled soldier, she about-faced and marched down the corridor, returning five minutes later with a basket full of supplies. 'I've put some infant formula in and two babies' bottles, in case she has trouble feeding. One is for the other child. Make sure the water is boiled, especially if we lose the mains. There's enough other food in there to keep you going for a few days. This, I'm afraid, is the best I can do.

'Now then, be back here first thing with that wheelbarrow of yours. It will make a fine pram and I'll see what else I can find for you.' The walls shook again when another explosion happened somewhere nearby. 'Be assured, Emma is in excellent hands.'

'Will you be leaving?' Artōrius asked. 'If the Russians come?'

'Someone has to stay with the patients,' she said, as a glint of fear registered in her eyes before hiding again behind her disagreeable persona.

'Will you be alright?' asked Artōrius with genuine concern.

'Of course.'

'You're a brave and kind woman, thank you.'

'I'm nothing of the sort, pragmatic, that's all. Enough of this idle chatter, I have work to do.'

'I won't forget your generosity.'

The Red Army entered Brandenburg sometime that night. By the time Artōrius awoke and was ready to leave the flat for the hospital, they had already ransacked the banks, and paper money blew down the streets like confetti. They must have thought the German currency was finished, as they showed no interest in it. Drunken Russian soldiers were smashing shop windows and looting whatever of value they could find. Seeing the money, Artōrius was torn between scavenging or going straight to the hospital. He decided that, to survive, they would need some money, so delayed his trip to the hospital to gather what he could. He returned to the flat five times with his pockets filled with cash, telling Emma to hide the loot and to keep the door locked on each visit. Unbeknown to Artōrius, his comings and goings had been observed.

Russian soldiers were in the hospital when he arrived and paid no attention to him as he walked the corridors, checking the rooms for Amelia. 'In here,' he heard a very weary matron call. Inside, a tired but beaming Amelia sat on one of the four beds with her newborn baby wrapped in a bundle and held in her arms. 'She will need plenty of rest for the next two or three days and other than that, mother and daughter are well.' A Red Army soldier poked his head in the room and, seeing the new baby, smiled and kept walking. 'Here,' the matron said, pointing to a cardboard box filled with more provisions. 'Can you carry it?'

'Of course.' Artōrius smiled. 'Come with us.'

'My duty is here.'

Outside, Artōrius placed the box in the wheelbarrow, making a nest on top of it for the new arrival. On their short walk back to the flat, it was clear any remaining semblance of law and order had evaporated. Had it not been for the baby asleep in the barrow, he felt sure they would have been robbed of the food.

Artōrius knew something was wrong the moment he saw the flat door was open. When they went in, Emma didn't need to say what had happened because her expression said all that needed to be said. Amelia ran and wrapped her arms about Emma, whispering, 'It's alright, you're safe now.'

'No, I'm not alright.' Unwrapping herself from Amelia's embrace, Emma held up her bloodied hands; an oozing red stain was coming through the dress. She had been stabbed. Emma let herself slump to the floor. 'Take care of Jacinta for me,' she pleaded to Amelia.

'Yes, of course, but you'll be OK. I know you will,' Amelia sobbed. 'Please Artōrius, save her. I know you can!'

'Here.' Emma pulled out the contact information for England that she had previously shown Amelia from the matchbox. 'They won't let you go to England because you're German, but I can go. Call this number and tell them you're Emma Kowalska. They've never seen me, so they won't know the difference. You already have my identity documents, and we could easily pass for each other. Please, Amelia, raise Jacinta as your own, but you must become Emma Kowalska and leave Germany.' She coughed and a trickle of blood formed in the corner of her mouth. 'Keep my shame secret.'

'Artōrius, please.'

Amelia sat beside Emma, cradling her in her arms. 'You have nothing to be ashamed of,' she whispered. 'I owe my life to you. When I was about to fall, you refused to let me go. You were willing to die with me. I swear on my father's grave that Emma Kowalska will live on and I will protect and raise Jacinta as my daughter in England. Your secret is safe.'

Choking out her words, Emma said, 'Thank you,' Then, seeing Amelia's baby for the first time, she smiled and asked, 'What are you going to call your child?'

'I was going to name her Jacinta, so I would never forget you. Now...' But as she spoke, Emma's breathing became shallower, then slowed, and finally stopped.

'Help me, Artōrius,' Amelia cried out, hugging Emma tightly.

The old man bent down and kissed Emma tenderly on the cheek before peacefully closing her eyelids. 'I'm sorry,' he whispered without Amelia hearing.

Crying, Amelia looked to the heavens and prayed that Emma was at peace with her maker. As her spirit passed, the new Emma Kowalska was born.

CHAPTER 16

Artōrius

'Who's there?' Emma called from her care home bed. Though the clock read two in the morning, but strangely she wasn't frightened.

'You don't remember me?' the male voice said with a chuckle.

'The voice is familiar,' she croaked, half asleep. 'Come into the light where I can take a better look at you.' The figure moved towards her and she sat up in bed. 'Have you come to take me?' she asked without alarm.

'No, my precious friend.'

'Then how can it be you haven't changed after all these years?'

'You remember me, then?'

'One doesn't easily forget those times.'

'Do you recall what I said before we parted?'

'That you would always look out for me. I remember those words clearly, because from time to time, I was certain I saw you—always in the distance, then vanishing into the crowd. I would shake my head and tell myself, "Don't be silly." It always happened when I needed to remember my promise. You gave me the strength to push through the difficult times we all face. Was it really you?'

'What do you think?'

'Then I wasn't sure, but now I see you. It seems impossible, yet I know it had to be.' She stretched her arms toward the man. Artōrius embraced her, holding Emma as she wept. 'I don't know why I'm crying,' she whispered. 'I can't seem to stop myself.'

Artōrius said nothing, waiting for Emma's tears to stop. Wiping her eyes, she asked, 'Why now? If not to take me, what else is it you want?'

'I've come for the ring.' He nodded towards her finger as he spoke. 'The one your father gave you, do you remember, when you were a little girl?'

'I've always suspected it was special. Sometimes it would shine with a brilliant gold, while at other times it took on a dull brass colour. It has fit like a glove my entire life, but recently, it's started to feel a little looser.'

'That's because the ring knows the time has come for it to leave, and me with it.' Artōrius held out his hand.

Emma removed the ring and gave it to him, saying, 'Before you leave, Artōrius, please tell me about it.'

It seeks those of a pure heart. When given in love, Artōrius and the ring travel with the wearer. Your father loved you as only a father can, and you loved Jacinta as a mother should. You have been a worthy custodian, and I honour you for that. Do not fear death; it is as your father imagined. But your time has not yet come.'

Artōrius smiled. 'I have one more surprise in store for you and I'm sorry I have waited so long. It will mean, however, that you have a hard decision to make.'

'Is it about the truth?'

'Yes.'

'I knew this day would come.'

'Indeed.'

'What would you do, Artōrius?'

'That's not for me to say.'

'In the wisdom of your years and as my guardian angel, what would you do?'

Artōrius thought for a moment. 'Some things are best left unspoken, but if the truth is out, then others may judge that decision harshly.'

Emma thought for a moment before saying, 'Jacinta found the letters?'

'Yes, my child, all but one.'

Emma reached for her pendant and gripped it in her hand.

Artōrius nodded.

'What should I do?' Emma asked.

Ignoring her question, Artōrius handed Emma the missing love letter dated August 1944. As she opened it and recognised her handwriting, the memories came flooding back and she was taken back in time.

It was Peter Kramer's last day in Dresden before returning to the front. He'd made love to his beautiful Amelia that morning and, in the early afternoon sun, as they walked along the river bank, he couldn't bear the thought of being parted from her.

Taking Amelia's hand, he led her back to the steps of the Lutheran church of Our Lady where, only days before, they had kissed for the first time as sweethearts. Standing together in silence on the steps, he let go of her hand and took from his pocket a silver 5 Reichsmark coin he had cut into two pieces. Placing half in her hand, he dropped to one knee and said, 'Amelia Huber, will you marry me?'

Looking at her coin and seeing the other part in his hand, she said, 'Yes, oh, yes, my dearest Peter. I will marry you.'

As he stood, she threw her arms about him and they embraced, holding each other tightly, frightened to let go. When they did, from his pocket, Peter took a piece of string and threaded it through a hole, punched in the half coin. As he hung it around Amelia's neck, he said, 'Amelia Huber, I have no engagement ring, but wear this as a symbol of my enduring love, in the knowledge I wear the other half and together we are as one.' She kissed him gently.

When Peter had threaded the other half coin, Amelia took it from him and, as she placed it around his neck, repeated his words, 'Peter Kramer, my precious man, wear this as a symbol of my enduring love, in the knowledge I wear the other half and together we are as one.' As Peter leaned forward to kiss her, Amelia stopped him and, holding her silver coin, said, 'Peter Kramer, this is my solemn vow and promise to you. No matter what happens, there will only be you and I will never take this off, not even at death.'

'I promise,' Peter mouthed and, pulling Amelia to him, they kissed.

Emma, without reading the letter, put it back into its envelope and sighed.

'Will I see you again?' she asked Artōrius.

'No, my friend, our time together is coming to an end. However, tomorrow, as my parting gift, you will awaken from this dream feeling renewed.'

Artōrius leaned down and kissed Emma gently on her forehead. 'Now sleep, my Guinevere,' he whispered.

CHAPTER 17

Truth

Armed with the package from Peter Kramer containing a present for Mother, I drove to the care home, pondering how to introduce the gift. Should I mention meeting Peter in the USA? I ultimately decided against it. Instead, I would simply give her the gift and wait to see her reaction.

It was a day of surprises. First, Mother greeted me at the front door, bright, mobile and confident in her balance. She even managed, with her arms outstretched, to spin around. Although it was executed carefully, it was a "look at me" moment.

'You're looking so well, Mother and in good spirt, too.'

'Do you know, Jacinta, I think I had stopped eating properly and, being on my own, became a little depressed. The company, activities, and meals here have done me a world of good, as you can see. Let's go to the lounge, and you can tell me all about your trip to the States.'

We were the only ones in the communal sitting room. 'I've got something for you,' I said, and handed her the package. She looked at me, silent but clearly articulating the unspoken words: 'What is it?'

'It's a gift from someone, for looking after the letters between Amelia and Peter.' I didn't know how she would react and, despite her stern look, it seemed as if she had been waiting for this.

'Have you looked at it?'

'No,' I answered.

'Do you know what it is?'

'No.'

'Can I take your vagueness as a sign that you will not tell me who gave it to you?'

Like mother, like daughter, I mumbled to myself.

Giving Mother a warm, thoughtful smile, I said, 'I'm going to take a walk. It's entirely up to you whether you want to share it with me.'

'Stay, Jacinta.' Carefully, Mother opened the package, revealing a small jewellery box. I had thought she knew its contents, but I was mistaken. As she lifted the lid and glanced inside, her mouth fell open in shock, dumbstruck by what she saw. Tears welled in her eyes and began to trickle down her cheeks as she removed the object from the box. When she lifted it free, I saw it was a pendant. Looking closer, I realised it was the matching half of the silver 5 Reichsmark coin she always wore—a sign of her enduring love for my father.

I couldn't believe my eyes. It made no sense to me. How could Peter Kramer possibly have the matching piece to Mother's wedding ring—my father's ring?

'Please, Jacinta, tell me who gave this to you?'

'Peter Kramer. I know the letters and records you kept in the shoebox showed he was killed in the war. But he wasn't. It was a mistake, a grave error. I found him through an online forum. That's why I went to the USA, to meet Peter Kramer. He gave this to me for you, but I don't understand.'

From inside her pocket, Mother produced a tattered envelope and I could see that it was one of the "Love letters from Dresden". I had to be mistaken, but it looked like the one that was missing.

Mother, with tears still falling, handed it to me. 'I'm not sure what to say, but this may help explain.'

'Have you read it?'

'Not in a very long time, but I know what it says because I wrote it, my love.' She sighed. 'It's a long story and I know this is going to come as a shock, but my real name is Amelia Huber. There is so much more I have to tell you, but please read the letter first.'

August 1944

Dearest Peter

Nothing could have prepared me for the emptiness I felt when you left after our week together. My body aches all over and I cry myself to sleep each and every night. If it wasn't for the silver coin I wear around my neck and knowing you have the other half, I would have surely died. Remember my promise to you, my beautiful man, I will never take it off, not even when I die, for it will be buried along with me. We are one and never will there be anyone else.

As agreed, I haven't told momma or papa that we are engaged, but I want to shout it from every corner, Peter Kramer is going to marry Amelia Huber and they will have 100 children.

I've just read what I've written and it sounds childish for an engaged woman, but perhaps the innocence of a child's voice is the purest way of telling you how much I love you. There is nothing else in my life but you.

Please stay safe, my love.

I love you

Amelia

I read the letter several times, trying to piece together all the information before I spoke. "I have so many questions," was the best I could manage. Then I added, 'Do you mind if I step outside for some fresh air?' As I turned to leave the room, a nurse entered, holding a portable phone. 'There's a call for you, Emma,' she said. My mind swirling with confusion, I continued to walk past her.

'Jacinta,' I heard my mother call for the third time as she summoned me back to the sitting room. Then she yelled excitedly, 'Peter, Peter Kramer, is coming here tomorrow, after all this time.'

'Mother, I don't understand any of this.' For the next two hours, I sat spellbound as she shared her story, growing up and falling in love with Peter, becoming pregnant, believing him killed, fleeing Dresden after the bombing, losing her identity papers, meeting Emma Kowalska and her daughter, Jacinta. How Emma had saved her life and, finally, the promise she made when Emma was fatally stabbed in Brandenburg. Mother was brought to tears retelling the story, and I cried with her. We both wept openly as she recounted losing Emma's Jacinta to tuberculosis caused by the hardships endured in the immediate aftermath of the war. She told of trying to keep me alive, before securing a passage to Britain through the contact Emma had given her.

That night, alone in bed, I wondered which of the Jacinta's really died. My birth certificate wasn't true. A DNA test would easily determine if Mother was telling the truth, and I was Amelia's daughter and not an orphan of war.

Who am I?

In my own musings, I had inadvertently answered the question, 'Is Mother telling the truth?' Emma had always been my mother, and nothing—not even a DNA test—could change that. That was the undeniable truth. There was no point in chasing shadows, as the outcome would always remain the same. Mother was my mother, regardless of genetics.

At that moment, I decided, once Peter and Mother had passed on, I would write their love story, even though that would mean revealing the real Emma Kowalska and her story.

EPILOGUE

Artōrius took me from my custodian, Amelia Huber, at the care home and, after kissing her tenderly on the forehead, we were gone from her life forever. In its truest meaning, she had been a worthy Guinevere and champion of love.

In telling her story to Jacinta, Amelia never spoke of Artōrius or the circumstances in Poland which caused Emma to flee. She also never talked of me, the ring, and nor did Jacinta notice I was gone from her mother's hand.

My next suitor was a young man in his late teens, in need of guidance, for Artōrius understood his path would be difficult. My initial sparkle caught his attention, and with great anticipation, he picked me up. However, after a brief inspection, he concluded I held no inherent value and discarded me like so many apple cores, tossing me into a field. I travelled with Artōrius to London, where, unceremoniously; I was left on a soiled table in a food hall, beneath a used McDonald's hamburger wrapper.

Keva fought back tears as she plopped herself down, brushing away the rubbish on the table to make room for the book she was reading. Her hands disturbed me from my hiding place, setting me spinning into her line of sight. When I finally settled back on the table, Keva picked me up, turning me over in her fingers and exploring my dull, brass-like surface. She polished me against her dress, then examined my facade once more. To her, I was still just a worthless piece of metal, but as she clasped me tightly in her hand, I could feel that she sensed there was something more.

But you don't want to know about Keva. It's Amelia and Peter that keeps you reading. They were, of course, now known as Peter and Emma.

I would love to say that Peter and Emma were finally reunited after sixty-six years apart, and that the love that brought them together as children had not diminished over the years. In fact, their desire to be with each other only grew stronger, fuelled by the knowledge that their time was limited. In a fairy tale world, they would have been married three months later, and at the wedding, rather than rings, the priest would bless two halves of a silver Reichsmark coin. These halves would then be exchanged during the ceremony, at the moment when couples typically give and receive rings—a symbol of their eternal love for one another. But life isn't like that.

What actually happened?

The deep love that Amelia and Peter held for each other in their memories remained alive when they reunited after their long absence. Inside, a part of them mourned for the years that had been lost, and they dreamed of cherishing the precious time they had left together. In reality, Peter Kramer and Emma Kowalska lived in different countries. Even for young people in love, marrying and being granted citizenship in a foreign country can be challenging; for the elderly, often deemed dependent or a financial burden, it's nearly impossible. With the right support, they believed that their story of lost love could have created an exception. However, to be together, they would have to tell the truth.

Peter would have to confess to his friends, patients, and colleagues that he lied about his heritage. For a man of integrity, this would have been a troublesome burden. For Amelia, it would be that she stole Emma Kowalska's identity to gain entry to England. At the very heart of it, Amelia would be forced to break the promise she'd made to Emma. What of Jacinta? The words of Artōrius had rung loudly in Amelia's mind. Some things are best left unspoken.

What is love, then? It is when the needs of others take precedence.

For Amelia and Peter to be together—nothing could prevent their love—they would have to hurt others, and neither could contemplate that. As a couple longing to be together, their time would have to wait for a higher calling.

Once, there were five "Love Letters from Dresden," but now there are many more.

THE END

Appendix

The Love Letter from Amelia to Peter
August 1944

August 1944

Liebster Peter,

nichts konnte mich auf die Leere vorbereiten, die ich spürte, als du mich nach unserer gemeinsamen Woche verlassen hast. Mein gesamter Körper schmerzt und ich weine mich jede Nacht in den Schlaf. Hätte ich nicht die silberne Münze um meinen Hals und wüsste ich nicht, dass du die andere Hälfte trägst, würde ich qualvoll zugrunde gehen. Stets erinnere ich mich an das Versprechen an meinen wunderschönen Mann, dass ich diese Kette niemals ablegen werde. Und wenn ich sterbe, will ich damit begraben werden. Wir sind eins und niemals wird es einen anderen geben.

Wie besprochen habe ich weder Mama noch Papa erzählt, dass wir verlobt sind, doch ich will es von allen Dächern rufen: Peter Kramer heiratet Amelia Huber und sie werden 100 Kinder bekommen!

Gerade habe ich noch einmal gelesen, was ich geschrieben habe und es klingt wirklich kindisch für eine verlobte Frau. Doch vielleicht ist die unschuldige Stimme eines Kindes der reinste Weg, dir zu sagen, wie sehr ich dich liebe. An meinem Leben zählst nur du.

Pass auf dich auf, mein Liebster

Ich liebe dich

Amelia

Emma Kowalska – World War Two Polish Identity Document

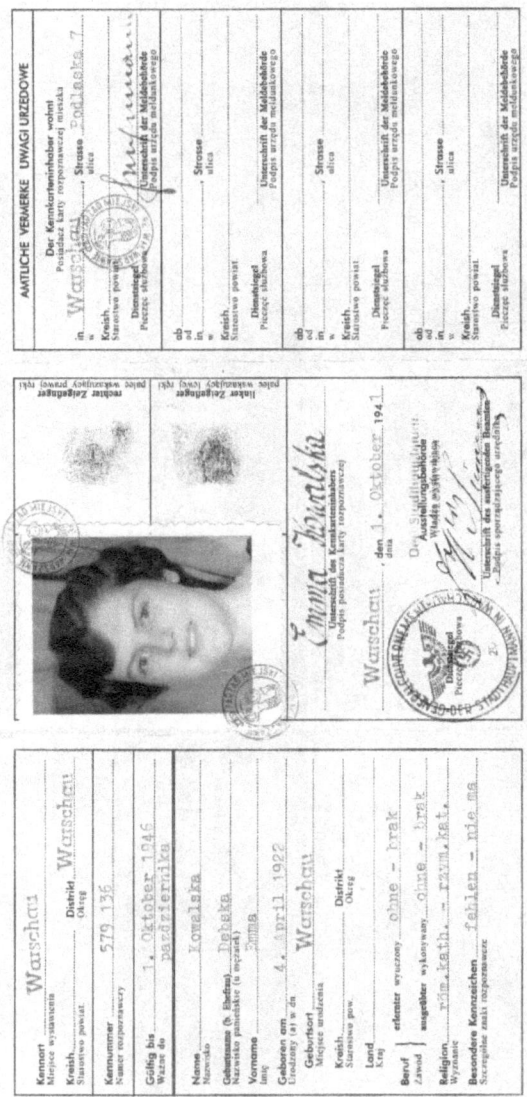

Half of the silver 1936 Reichsmark Coin worn by Amelia Huber

Amelia Huber
1945

Peter Kramer 1944

Jacinta Kowalska in search of her mother's story.
Dresden

Silent Trail
Book #2 Artōrius Series

Inspired by our trek across Spain and the people we met on the "Way of St. James," *Silent Trail* is a spy mystery set along the renowned Camino de Santiago.